Beverly Gray, Junior

Anselo stopped close to the window and continued his playing.

(BEVERLY GRAY, JUNIOR)

BEVERLY GRAY
JUNIOR

By CLAIR BLANK

GROSSET & DUNLAP
Publishers   NEW YORK

The Beverly Gray College Mystery Series

CONTENTS

Contents

CHAPTER I

Return

"THE MEETING will please come to order!" Lenora Whitehill, the newly elected president of the Alpha Delta Sorority, called.

The words could scarcely be heard above the din of chatter and laughter that emanated from the group of girls gathered in the college dormitory room.

"I demanded order!" the president said again, louder this time.

"And what did you get?" Lois Mason asked laughingly.

"Some disrespectful giggles," Lenora answered. "Hereafter when I, as the president of this august assemblage, demand order I want—order."

"Hear! Hear!" Shirley Parker said in applause.

The three remaining girls, Beverly Gray, Anne

White, and Rosalie Arnold, faced the president obediently.

The six were gathered in the room shared by Beverly and Shirley in Chadwick Hall. It was a cheerful room, indicative of the fun-loving, merry girls who lived in it. There were pictures and gay pennants hung on the walls, bright cushions were scattered about on bed and chairs, books and magazines with their covers spattered with pictures and colors were strewn about on desks and even on the window sill. A slight breeze stirred the ruffled curtain at the window where the warm September sun shone in.

The girls had returned this very morning from their various summer vacations to begin the third year of their college life. The Alpha Delta Sorority, which met on the first and last day of every term, also when any member called a special meeting, promptly convened in Beverly's and Shirley's room.

"What do you want order for?" Lois asked a trifle suspiciously. "Are you going to make a speech?"

Lenora beamed. "That is the idea!"

"I'm leaving," Lois said. However, she remained in her comfortable position on Beverly's bed, making no effort to put her words into effect. Lenora and Lois were the two madcaps in the sorority. They inevitably tried to outdo each other with wisecracks and teasing. Each was fully aware, however, that the other scarcely meant a word of what she said. Their teasing was all in the spirit of fun, and as such it was accepted by the other members of the organization.

"Let's hear the speech," Beverly said resignedly.

"Yes, let's get it over with," Shirley added.

"Woe is me," Lois murmured tragically and, leaning back on the pillows, covered her face with a magazine. "I refuse to listen to any speech. It's too hot."

Lenora was unperturbed by the attitude of her classmates. Nothing could disturb her equilibrium. She was sublimely unaware of Lois's disgusted attitude and the laughing expectancy of the other girls.

"This year," she began impressively, "we are juniors."

"You're telling us," came from Lois.

"We have a big responsibility on our shoulders," continued Lenora. "We have to set an example for the freshmen and sophomores."

"Poor kids," came sympathetically from under the magazine.

"It is up to us to convey by our actions the high

ideals and good sportsmanship for which Vernon College stands."

"Rah! Rah!" applauded Lois.

"It is up to us to see that they fully realize what an honor it is to be students at Vernon."

"An honor for which we are all duly grateful," concluded Lois, the irrepressible.

"Last term two of our good friends, Gerry Foster and Mickey Mowre, graduated," Lenora said again, "to fare forth into the cold, cruel world. They left behind them hopes and wishes that we may hold high the banner of Vernon."

"Hear ye! Hear ye!" was the mischievous interruption.

"All of us," Lenora said, after an exasperated glance in her friend's direction, "have a desire to leave stepping stones on the path of our college life. We——"

"We hope to——" interrupted Lois but was checked.

"Do you want to make my speech for me?" demanded Lenora.

"Sure," Lois said promptly. She scrambled up from her reclining position. "Ladies," she began theatrically, "I propose that we adjourn this business meeting."

"I second the motion," Shirley said quickly.

"And we are all in favor," Anne agreed.

"We will adjourn to Weller's," continued Lois, "where we will indulge our esthetic tastes in sweets."

"Meeting is adjourned!" Lenora declared with vigor. She was an ardent fan of Weller's, and nothing could be allowed to interfere with a chance to visit the favorite ice-cream saloon of the college students.

"After dinner tonight," Rosalie proposed, "let's have our fortunes told."

"With what?" Lenora demanded.

"Haven't you heard?" Rosalie asked. "A band of gypsies have camped on the outskirts of the town. Let's visit them."

"That would be fun!" Anne agreed.

"They came in their covered wagons," Rosalie continued. "They're dressed just like you see them in the movies—gold rings in their ears an' everything."

CHAPTER II

The Gypsies

DINNER at Chadwick Hall was over, and the six Alphas assembled on the porch of the Hall. Other girls were seated on porch railings and steps. One of their number had a ukulele, and the girls sang as she strummed out popular melodies. The sun was setting, and the long autumn twilight hovered over the eastern horizon. It would be hours yet before darkness came on, and the girls could enjoy themselves out of doors on this, their last night before studies began.

The Alphas were on their way to the gypsy camp; that is, they had started out with that intention, but Lenora was deeply involved in the recitation of the latest popular song.

As the chorus came to an end, Lois grabbed her friend's arm. "For goodness' sake, come along. We want to get started before dark."

"Don't rush me," Lenora said with maddening slowness. "Don't forget," she called over her shoulder to the girl with the ukulele who had been singing with her, "the word of that last line is 'with' not 'for.'"

"Of all the slow-pokes," Lois was storming when they joined the other girls, "you take the cake."

"Now, I ask you," Lenora appealed, "why should we hurry? Time is plentiful, and I don't believe in rushing."

"I can see that," Lois said with sarcasm.

"Do you suppose we shall have to cross the gypsy's palm with silver before she will tell us anything?" Anne asked.

"Course we shall," Lenora said promptly. "I hope my fortune is good."

Perhaps we should take a little time now to acquaint our new readers with the girls of the Alpha Delta Sorority. First there is Beverly Gray, best loved and adored member, and her roommate, the rich, pleasant Shirley Parker. Then there is Anne White, the girl who comes from Beverly's home town of Renville, and her roommate, Lois Mason. The boisterous Lenora Whitehill rooms with quiet, unassuming Rosalie Arnold. The six girls had first become friends in their freshman year, when they started playing pranks on the upper classmen. They had organized into a sorority in their sophomore year at Vernon, when they helped to solve several mysteries in which they had become involved.

The girls continued on their way through the little town of Vernon with its stores, large, beautiful homes, and one movie theater, across the railroad tracks to the outskirts of the town.

"I wonder why they camped all the way over here across the train tracks," grumbled Lenora. "They might just as easily have moved closer, then we wouldn't have had to walk so far."

"Lazybones," chaffed Lois.

"The townspeople wouldn't hear of the gypsies' coming any closer," Rosalie informed them. "Gypsies are considered taboo by all the respectable citizens of Vernon."

"How do you know?" demanded Lenora of her roommate.

"Karl told me."

"Aha!" Lois and Lenora pounced on her. "Who is Karl?" they demanded sternly.

"The soda clerk at Weller's," Rosalie answered innocently. "Why?"

"So! That is the attraction at Weller's," Anne laughed.

"And I thought Rosalie went only for the banana splits," Lenora scoffed.

"Silly," Rosalie said flushing, "I don't go to Weller's to see him, if that is what you are hinting at."

"That is what you tell us," Lois murmured teasingly.

"I notice you go quite often yourself," Rosalie retorted.

Beverly and Shirley stepped into the breach to avert another argument.

"Look!" Shirley said. "There's the camp."

"They have a camp fire lit," added Beverly.

"Ahoy!" Lenora shouted waving her scarf.

"Stop it, you idiot!" Lois said sternly. "They will think they are being besieged by lunatics."

"Speak for yourself!" responded Lenora.

"Oooooooo," began Lois threateningly.

"Beverly, protect me," whimpered Lenora, putting Beverly between her and the vindictive Lois.

"Behave yourself and you won't need protection," said Beverly unfeelingly.

"Yes, ma'am," answered Lenora meekly, and thereafter walked along docilely beside Beverly.

The gypsy wagons were drawn up in a circle about the leaping camp fire. Men and women stood or sat and talked together. The women were garbed in flowing dresses of gay pattern, and the men wore brightly colored bandanas. The gold of the rings in their ears and the sparkling whiteness of their teeth gleamed against their dark skin. Several children were playing before the fire. In the background stood the horses which were used to draw the wagons when the gypsies were moving.

A tall, slender man detached himself from a group about one of the wagons and approached the girls as they came near the camp. He bowed low before them and flashed his teeth in a brilliant smile.

"The young ladies honor the gypsies. Do you wish to have the future read for you?"

"Yes," Beverly answered, speaking for the group.

"Only the future," added Lenora. "We know all about the past."

"If the young ladies will step this way, Orlenda, the oldest one of our tribe, who can look far into the future and see what is written on the cards, will tell you what is hidden in the mysterious veil of the days to come."

"Some line," Lenora murmured in a stage whisper to Lois.

"Hush," that individual said sternly. "He will hear you!"

The gypsy led the way to a wagon in the center

of the circle. An old woman, toothless and weather stained, sat on the steps smoking a disreputable pipe. She looked up with an evil grimace as the young women and the gypsy stopped before her.

"The pretties desire to have the cards read?" the gypsy woman smirked.

The man said something to her in a low undertone, and the smirk was replaced by a frown. She flung back angry words in a language the girls couldn't understand and stood up. She emptied her pipe with a vicious smack against the door of the wagon and buried it in a capacious pocket in her skirt.

"If the young ladies will step into the wagon——" the man hinted.

One by one the girls filed into the darkened interior. The woman had seated herself on a low stool behind a table. In her hand she held a pack of greasy cards. Her eyes were fixed on them, and she was crooning as she swayed wearily from side to side. She motioned to Lenora, and that young lady promptly took her place across the table from the gypsy.

"I see—a blond young man, one who has much money. For you I say—do not talk too much—listen."

"Oh, boy," chortled Lois. "That's good! Telling Lenora not to talk too much! Ho-ho!"

The girls had difficulty in smothering Lois's mirth so they could hear the rest of Lenora's fortune. After Lenora, Rosalie was motioned forward. She received much the same forecast as had Lenora. Then Anne and Lois stepped up to receive their reading. Shirley was told she would some day be a great actress, and as that was the secret dream she cherished, she was delighted.

When Beverly's turn came, the gypsy shook her head forebodingly. She mumbled to herself, and the girls exchanged startled glances.

"You will have a dark period in your life. You will be in great danger. It will cause much worry to your loved ones."

"What will the danger be?" asked Beverly.

"That Orlenda cannot tell you, but it will be great, it will be soon. There will be a dark young man in your life. I see two, three men—each one loves you."

"Gracious!" Lenora murmured.

"Will these men be associated with the danger?" Beverly asked interestedly.

The gypsy nodded. "But the dark clouds will pass. The sun will shine again, and you shall return to your friends." She rose and swept the cards into a heap. "That is all Orlenda can tell you tonight."

"Oh, gee," Lenora murmured dissatisfiedly as the girls left the wagon. "She should tell us more than that for our fifty cents."

"Imagine Beverly," Lois laughed. "Three men in her life! Whoops, my dear!"

"She has been hiding something from us," Shirley declared, laughing. "Out with it, Beverly!"

"Don't tell me you believe all the stuff the gypsy told you," Beverly laughed. "I'll bet she made up half of it."

"I hope not," Lenora said promptly. "I rather like what she told me, and I hope——"

"I especially like the part where she said Lenora talked too much," Lois giggled ecstatically.

"She didn't say I talked too much," Lenora defended. "She just warned me not to talk but to listen."

"Same thing," Lois declared.

"It isn't!" Lenora said firmly.

"I didn't like what the gypsy said about Beverly," Shirley said frowning. "It wasn't very promising."

"It was—gloomy," Anne added.

"Nonsense." Beverly laughed away their fears. "I don't believe half of it."

"She said there was danger," Shirley continued.

"From what, for instance?" Beverly demanded. "What could possibly happen here in Vernon?"

"She is right," Lenora declared to the others. "Nothing ever happens here. I am afraid we shall all wilt away this year. There is not the promise of the least excitement."

"Let's have a banana split before we go to the Hall," Rosalie suggested.

"So you can talk to Karl?" demanded Lenora mischievously.

"Oh, go away," Rosalie said with dignity. "You talk to the clerk just as much as I do."

So the girls picked their way carefully across the railroad tracks, teasing and laughing as they entered Weller's. It was growing late, and they had to hurry. The sun had entirely disappeared from view, and the stars were coming out in countless numbers. The moonlight was irregular, drifting often from behind dark clouds.

"It's going to rain," predicted Shirley.

"Let it rain," said Lenora unconcerned.

The girls were crossing the campus. They had fallen silent, strange as it may seem, and not a sound disturbed the silence. Suddenly Shirley, who had been walking ahead with Lois, stopped and warned the others to make no noise. She pointed across the campus, where a slinking figure could be seen stealing from Chadwick Hall. It was a man, and as he came suddenly into the momentary brilliant light from the moon they saw that he was dark and swarthy.

"A gypsy!" Lenora murmured excitedly.

"What do you suppose he is after?" whispered Rosalie.

"He isn't after anything," Beverly answered. "It rather looks as if he had what he wanted and is leaving."

"Do you suppose he has stolen anything?" Anne asked wide-eyed.

"Course he has," Lenora said promptly. "A gypsy wouldn't miss the chance."

"What shall we do?" Rosalie asked frantically. "Call the police?"

"What police?" Lois asked sarcastically. "We would have to run all the way back to town, and then he would probably be gone."

"We have to catch him," Beverly said.

"We'll surround him," Shirley proposed.

"He has something in his hand," Anne pointed out.

"Probably the stolen goods," Lois answered.

"We'll get it," Lenora said determinedly.

CHAPTER III

Disappearance

ONE BY ONE the girls spread out, keeping in the shadows, until they formed an invisible circle about the man. Then one by one they stepped out into the light where he could see them.

"What do you want here?" Beverly demanded.

"Nothing," was the surly answer. The man took in the sight of the girls in position all about him. "I have done nothing."

"What have you in your hand?" Shirley demanded.

"Nothing."

"What a silly answer," Lenora laughed. "We can see you have something. What did you steal?"

"Nothing," the man repeated stubbornly, at the same time edging farther backward.

The girls closed in farther, but they were not prepared for the sudden rush he made, completely bowling over two of their members. Beverly and Shirley flung themselves on him and succeeded only in knocking whatever it was he carried in his hand to the ground. The man disappeared into the shadows, running toward the gypsy camp.

Lenora and Lois picked themselves up from where he had knocked them on the grass.

"I'm mortified," Lenora declared.

"Me too," Lois said woefully. "We let the villain escape."

"But look what we have." Shirley held up what the man had dropped.

The girls crowded eagerly around. Shirley carefully unwound the bandana handkerchief and exposed a roll of money and some jewelry.

"Gracious!" Rosalie said excitedly.

"Where do you suppose he got all that money?" Anne demanded.

"He must have robbed the safe in Mrs. Dennis' office," Lois concluded.

"Let's take this in to her," Beverly proposed.

"Will she be surprised!" prophesied Lenora gleefully. "We stopped the thief from making off with her cash."

Mrs. Dennis was more than surprised. She was astounded. Together with the girls she went to her office, and there they beheld the little safe broken open and papers scattered about in confusion. The man had taken all the money in sight. Some of the girls gave their jewelry to Mrs. Dennis to keep in the safe for them; this too the gypsy had taken. Thanks to the Alpha Delta members the money and the jewelry were restored to their owners.

Mrs. Dennis reported the attempted robbery to the police in Vernon but was informed that the gypsies had already begun to move. They had broken camp, and their wagons were seen lumbering through the streets of the town, apparently headed south.

"It is just as well," Beverly said. "We couldn't identify the man for certain, because in the darkness we didn't get a very clear view of his face."

"But we would know his voice," Lenora pointed out.

"Oh, well," Shirley said philosophically, "he didn't get anything, so we needn't worry."

The girls scattered then, each going to her room. Beverly sat down to write letters home, and Shirley buried herself in a book. The minutes ticked silently away, and finally Beverly laid down her pen.

"I think I'll run down and mail these letters," she said rising.

"It's going to rain," cautioned Shirley with a languorous glance out the window.

"I'll be back in a jiffy," Beverly promised. "Want to come along?"

"No, I'd rather stay here and read," Shirley answered. "This book is good, and I'm in the most exciting part."

Beverly laughed. "Is the villain pursuing the heroine?"

"Yep," Shirley answered, "and, ooooo, he is a villainish villain."

When Beverly had departed, Shirley continued to read until the hero had satisfactorily outwitted the villain and rescued the heroine. Then she laid down the book and slipped into comfortable pajamas. She knelt by the open window and looked out over the campus. Clouds were hiding the moon again, and the promise of rain was strong in the air. A glance at her tiny wrist watch showed her that it was almost ten o'clock. So late! It was over an hour since Beverly had gone out to mail her letters. What could be keeping her?

Beverly must have been waylaid by Lenora or Lois, Shirley decided. Almost any of the girls in Chadwick Hall might have called her into her room for a moment. Beverly had an army of friends here at college. She was the most popular girl on the campus. And yet, for all of her popularity, she wasn't in the least conceited. Nor was she of the goody-goody type. Beverly would enter into anything that promised fun.

Shirley considered herself lucky to be Beverly's roommate. Any of the other girls would gladly have changed places with her. Beverly was her best friend, and Shirley made no secret of the fact that anything Beverly did was all right with her. Ever since Beverly, in her freshman year, had rescued Shirley from the fire that had destroyed the first Chadwick Hall, the rich girl had worshiped her. Shirley had been selfish and egotistical that first year at Vernon, and yet Beverly had set about patiently and kindly to win a friendship that would last forever. Personally, Shirley could never **understand** what it had been that made Beverly stick to her that first term. Surely she, Shirley, had been everything a pleasant roommate should not be. She had never been friendly with Beverly, and yet the impulsive, lovable Beverly had stayed with her. She had overlooked the slights and sneers that Shirley had showered on her, and in return had given nothing but gentle kindness and quick forgiveness.

Rain was drifting against the window, and Shirley rose and closed it. If Beverly didn't hurry, she would certainly get wet. Shirley settled herself in bed with a magazine. Might as well read **until** Beverly came in. The clock ticked on, hour after hour. The printed page became more and more difficult for Shirley to see. She yawned prodigiously and decided to have a cat-nap before Beverly returned.

The cat-nap stretched into a dreamless sleep. It was morning when Shirley awoke, a gray, rainy, cheerless morning. The clouds that hung low over the college were heavy and leaden. Rain streamed against the windowpanes and pattered on the roof. The very air was damp and chill. It was difficult for Shirley to rise; she would much rather have stayed snug and warm in bed. A glance at Beverly's bed brought the red-headed girl upright in a second. The bed had not been slept in. That meant Beverly had not returned to the Hall at all last night. Mentally Shirley rebuked herself for falling asleep, though what good would it have done had she stayed awake? Shirley made record time in dressing and bounded across the hall into Anne and Lois' room before those worthy ones were even out of bed.

"Ye gods," Lois chirped when Shirley appeared, "look what the rain dragged out of bed!"

"Beverly hasn't been in her room all night," Shirley informed them worriedly.

"What?" The statement brought both Anne and Lois tumbling from the covers.

"She went out to mail some letters last night, and she didn't come back," Shirley continued.

"Have you told Mrs. Dennis?" Lois demanded.

"No," Shirley admitted.

"Perhaps she can explain it," Anne said hopefully.

"I'll go see her now," Shirley said, and departed on a run.

But Mrs. Dennis had no explanation to offer regarding Beverly's absence. She was as surprised as Shirley had been, and as worried. At breakfast the other girls were questioned, but none could shed any light on Beverly's strange behavior. It was a mystery. Why should Beverly stay away from the Hall all night?

Much as they didn't want to, the girls had to go to classes on this their first day. They endeavored to keep a cheerful countenance and declared that Beverly would return today sometime with an explanation. At lunch time Beverly was the sole topic of conversation, and everyone volunteered a different solution to the mystery of her absence. But Beverly did not return. Afternoon faded into evening, and still she did not return. After dinner the Alphas gathered in Shirley's room to discuss the subject.

"We have to find an explanation somehow,"

Lenora said frowning. "Never let it be said that a mystery stumped the Alpha Deltas."

"She couldn't have run away," Shirley said slowly.

"Why not?" Rosalie asked. "To me that is the only explanation."

"If she had—" Lois chimed in, "run away, I mean—she would have taken some of her things."

"That's true," Rosalie nodded. "If she didn't run away, what happened to her?"

"You're asking us," Lois said wearily.

"Maybe she decided to deliver the letters in person," Lenora said flippantly.

"Be serious," Shirley rebuked the mischievous Lenora. "I'm really worried. I can't understand it."

"Remember what the gypsy said," Rosalie continued slowly.

"What was that?" Shirley asked.

"She said Beverly would be in danger——"

"And it would cause much worry to her loved ones," Anne finished.

"Cheerful cherubs, you two," Lois declared.

"Maybe she has run off with one of the three men in her life," Lenora continued lightly.

"Nonsense," Shirley said shortly.

"Somehow," Lenora rose and stretched luxuriously, "I can't be worried yet. Beverly will pop up, wait and see. Nothing can keep that girl down."

"The gypsy said the clouds would pass and she would be returned to her friends," Anne reminded them.

"Gosh," Lois scoffed, "I hope you didn't believe anything that gypsy said!"

"Why not?" Rosalie demanded.

"Because she couldn't tell what was going to happen any more than I could," Lois answered. "She just has a good line of chatter and hands it out to anyone that will swallow it."

"But some of what she prophesied has come true," Rosalie pointed out in defense. "She said Beverly would be in danger——"

"How do we know she *is* in danger?" Lenora demanded. "We are making a wild guess."

"Probably getting worried over nothing," Lois agreed.

"I wish," Shirley said, "I had gone with her. She asked me to, but I wouldn't."

"Then neither one of you might have come back," said doubtful Rosalie.

"At least I would know what happened," Shirley pointed out. "I would at least know if she had been —hurt or——"

"Gosh," Lois said restlessly, "you all give me the jitters! Everybody is so cheerful!"

"Positive rays of sunshine," Lenora added. "Don't be so pessimistic," she urged the other girls. "We don't have to worry ourselves sick because Beverly didn't come home last night. She probably had a good reason for staying out. She will turn up tomorrow for sure."

"I hope so," Shirley finished. "If she doesn't turn up tonight, Mrs. Dennis is going to notify her parents. She went into town to talk to Inspector Dugan this afternoon."

"What did the Dean say?" questioned Lois.

"Miss Wilder was as worried as Mrs. Dennis. She could offer no explanation," Shirley said.

"Beverly certainly takes the cake for stirring up things," Lenora declared. "Every term something has happened to keep us excited."

"I only hope it is nothing serious this time," Shirley said fervently.

CHAPTER IV

Friends

THE HOURS and the days passed with no word of or from Beverly. The girls were worried. Even the two care-free madcaps, Lois and Lenora, were forced to admit that Beverly's disappearance was taking on an extremely serious aspect. They had a brief word of her from Inspector Dugan on the second day—that is, they thought it was of Beverly.

On the night Beverly disappeared there had been a robbery in Vernon. A man, believed to be a gypsy, had entered a little art shop and held up the proprietor. A girl answering Beverly's description had been in the shop at the time. The gypsy had taken a wrist watch from the girl and run out. The girl immediately gave chase. That was all the owner of the art shop could tell them. The girl had run from his store after the gypsy, and she had not returned. The gypsy had disappeared and the girl with him.

If it had been Beverly, the girls could understand why she had given chase. Beverly, above everything else, prized her wrist watch. It had been presented to her by the girls of Vernon when she rescued Shirley from the Hall fire. Nothing could ever make her part with it. Possibly she had had some idea of trapping the thief, but the girls could see how hopeless such a thing was. Beverly would have no chance with a strong, agile, desperate man. It had been sheer folly to attempt to stop him. Yet a girl of Beverly's impulsive nature would have made an attempt to retrieve something she prized very highly.

The girls, as well as the police, were puzzled. Where could Beverly have gone? She had gone out into the night and, literally, disappeared into thin air. What was the explanation of that?

Shirley and the other Alphas spent hours trying to figure out how and where Beverly could have gone.

"I give it up," Lois said at last. "Maybe I'm dumb, but I don't know what to think."

"You and me both," Lenora said promptly.

"What does Inspector Dugan think?" Anne asked Shirley.

As Beverly's roommate, Shirley was more privi-
leged than the rest. She it was went with Miss Wilder to see Inspector Dugan, and it was to her the
authorities turned for information about Beverly.
Shirley had to recount over and over again Beverly's doings on the night she disappeared, not only
to the police but to the other girls on the campus,
and to Beverly's parents, who were in daily com-
munication with Vernon.

"The inspector is afraid that—Beverly might
have been kidnaped," Shirley answered slowly.
"Lately there have been so many kidnapings in the
country that he is positive that is what happened
to Beverly."

"No one has demanded ransom," Lois pointed
out.

"He is sure that they will, sooner or later."

"Does Miss Wilder agree with him?" Anne
asked.

"Yes. In fact, that seems to be the common be-
lief of everybody," Shirley answered.

"Has he any idea who the kidnapers might be?"
Rosalie asked.

"He believes the gypsies are responsible," Shirley
answered. "He thinks that because Beverly ran
after the gypsy who robbed the art shop."

"Has he any clues?" Lenora asked interestedly.

"Clues?" Lois demanded. "What clues could he have?"

"How do I know?" Lenora shrugged. "Policemen are always supposed to look for clues."

"If he thinks it is the gypsies," Anne cut in, "why doesn't he go after them?"

"He has notified the police in all sections of the country to be on the watch for them," Shirley answered. "As soon as word comes to him where they are, he will go and search the camp."

"I'll bet Beverly's picture has been in every newspaper in the country," Lois declared. "The town of Vernon is overrun with reporters from every place."

"Yes," Shirley agreed. "Her father is an important something or other in the government, and Beverly's disappearance would create a sensation."

"Hi, Shirley, there is a man downstairs asking for you," a girl stuck her head in the door to give Shirley the information and promptly disappeared again.

"Probably Inspector Dugan," Shirley said, rising and crossing to the door. "I'll see you after he has gone and give you all the information he has—if any," she added.

But it was not Inspector Dugan who rose and advanced to meet Shirley as she entered the living room. It was a tall, good-looking young man, and Shirley immediately liked him. She especially liked his clear, honest, confident gray eyes and his wide, boyish smile. He wore a neat blue business suit and carried a soft felt hat in his hand.

"Miss—Shirley Parker?" he asked.

"Yes," Shirley said puzzled.

"I'm Jim Stanton. Perhaps you have heard of me?"

Of course she had. He was a good friend of Beverly's from Renville. Beverly had often spoken of him. He had graduated from Yale last June, and at present was looking for a position as an engineer.

They shook hands and sat down in two chairs drawn apart from the others.

"Mrs. Dennis had to rush off to Vernon for something or other," Jim explained, "or she would have introduced us. I only just arrived in town this morning. I'm staying at the Hotel Wildon, in Vernon."

"You've—come about Beverly?" Shirley asked.

"Yes. Her parents, needless to say, are very worried. I've been rather at loose ends lately, and since I'm a friend of Beverly's I thought I would run down here and see what I could do."

"There seems to be nothing anyone can do," Shirley answered. "The authorities know scarcely

anything. They are as completely in the dark as
we are."

"It is four days now since she disappeared, is it
not?" Jim continued.

"Yes," Shirley answered. The young man could
tell by the tense look on her face that they had
been four days of anxious strain. "She just walked
out of the art shop—and disappeared."

"Has any trace been found of the gypsies?" Jim
asked.

"No. I suppose you have read the whole story
in the papers?"

"Every word," Jim nodded. "Is Anne White
about anywhere?"

"Upstairs in her room. You know her from
home?"

"Yes, I'll talk to her later. I know she is a great
friend of Beverly's. How is she taking all this?"

"Just like the rest of us," Shirley answered. "We
are all waiting—hoping for some word."

"Tell me, what is the opinion about the school?
Do the girls think she—ran off?"

"No," Shirley answered honestly. "The girls and
the teachers seem to think she must have been kidnaped. We know of no reason why Beverly should
run away."

Jim frowned thoughtfully. "There has been absolutely no word of any kind?"

"None whatever. We have notified everyone we can think of. All the hospitals have been questioned, all——"

"If she had been in one of them we would have heard by now," Jim said. He brushed a microscopic bit of dust from his hat. "I came down here to help somehow to find her, but there seems to be no place to start."

"All the girls are aching to do something, too," Shirley said, "but we are at loose ends."

"I say, may I break up this meeting?" a gay voice inquired cheerfully.

Shirley looked up to see Larry Owens standing at her side. Readers of *Beverly Gray, Sophomore,* will remember Larry as the Secret Service aviator whom Beverly met while spying on a gang of smugglers. The young aviator had become friends with all the girls of the Alpha Delta Sorority, and especially Beverly.

Shirley introduced Jim and Larry, and the two young men solemnly shook hands. Mentally each decided that he liked the other. Shirley looked at the two straight, clean, strong young men and wondered what Beverly's faculty was for making such staunch friends. Both of these young fellows had come to offer their services in the search for the girl who was a friend to each. They were quite willing to dare anything if they might restore her to her parents and friends.

Larry immediately took command of the situation, as he always did, in his gay, care-free manner, and demanded the latest news of Beverly. Shirley supplied what little she had. For a while they talked together about possibilities and plans; then Shirley rose. It was almost time for dinner at Chadwick Hall, so the two young men left the Hall together. They walked down the tree-bordered college lanes to the city.

"Can you tell me a good hotel to put up at?" Larry asked. "I've set my plane down at the airport, but I haven't unloaded my bags yet."

"Why not come to the Hotel Wildon and bunk with me?" Jim proposed.

"Swell!" Larry said promptly, if inelegantly. "We are in the hunt for the same reason, so we might as well stick together."

And so Beverly, who might be hundreds of miles away, was responsible for bringing together these two young men who were to become firm friends and figure largely in her life.

CHAPTER V

A *Clue*

LENORA AND SHIRLEY were in Weller's sipping sodas when Jim and Larry next met them. The young men promptly availed themselves of the opportunity to chat and joined them. Lenora already knew Larry, but she had to be introduced to Jim.

For two days now the young men had been in Vernon. They had met Inspector Dugan and talked with him at great length regarding Beverly's mysterious disappearance, but they had learned nothing beyond that which they already knew.

"What's the latest reports?" Lenora asked.

"There is nothing new," Larry shrugged.

"We've just come from interviewing the art shop owner," Jim volunteered.

"Did you learn anything new?" Shirley wanted to know.

"That man doesn't know his own mind," Larry

scoffed. "Didn't you say the night she disappeared Beverly was wearing a white sports dress trimmed in blue?"

"Yes," affirmed both Lenora and Shirley together.

"Well, the owner of the art shop says now that the girl that was in his store at the time the gypsy entered was wearing a dress trimmed in red."

"He had better make up his mind to one color and stick to it," Lenora declared. "A few days ago he thought it was green."

"Maybe he is color blind," Larry laughed.

"Things look rather hopeless, don't they?" Shirley murmured, idly stirring her soda with the straws.

"Not at all," Larry said with far more confidence than he felt. "Mysteries always look hopeless, but something is bound to turn up sooner or later."

"Meanwhile, we have to waste time waiting," Lenora said restlessly.

"Inspector Dugan is doing all he can," Jim said slowly. "He has the police in every state on the lookout for the gypsies."

"If she is with the gypsies," Shirley said. "He is only making a guess at that. He might be on the wrong track entirely."

"It seems the most logical," Larry defended. "Both Beverly and the gypsies disappeared on the same night."

"But where did they go?" Lenora asked. "A band of gypsies couldn't vanish into thin air with their wagons and horses and all."

"These did," Shirley reminded her.

"It's funny," Jim agreed. "They were headed south when they left Vernon, and the southern roads are the ones being most carefully watched."

"If only we knew if she was all right," persisted Shirley gloomily, "if we were only sure they hadn't harmed her!"

The other three faces became thoughtfully grave. The thought had been in the mind of each one, but only Shirley had put it into words. There were gruesome tales of what kidnapers had done to their victims. They could only hope and pray that nothing like that would befall Beverly.

When the young people had finished their sodas they rose and turned toward the college. It was late in September, but the sun still shone down warmly on the friendly earth, and the leaves of the trees were turning slowly to golden and red. Girls in gayly colored dresses were strolling along the walks or standing and chatting beneath the trees. Some carried tennis racquets, as they came from the fine courts provided for the students. The windows of the college buildings were open, and curtains swayed gently in the breeze. Various girls were leaning out shouting conversation back and forth.

"Great school," Larry said nodding toward the college.

"The best," Lenora said promptly.

As the young people stopped at the entrance to the college grounds and the boys prepared to make their way back to Vernon, Lois came dashing madly up to them.

"Listen—news——" she panted.

Shirley gripped her arm. "Has some word come from Beverly?"

Lois shook her head and endeavored to catch her breath so she could impart her news.

"No, but Inspector Dugan—heard that——"

"Well, come on," Lenora said impatiently. "What did he hear?"

"I'm trying to tell you," Lois said painstakingly. "If you will give me a chance and not——"

"Lois!" Shirley said tensely. "Tell us——"

"Inspector Dugan has had word that the gypsies——"

"Yes?" Larry interrupted quickly.

"—are camped about five miles directly to the south."

"They are!" Jim echoed joyfully. "Larry! We are going places!"

"You said it that time, boy. We're traveling right now."

"Inspector Dugan has taken his car and some men and is already on his way," Lois volunteered.

"We'll take the *Red Bird*," Larry said. "Come along, Jim, we're headed for the airport."

"We'll be on pins and needles until you come back and tell us what you found," Lenora called.

"We wish you luck," Lois added.

The two young men departed quickly for the Vernon airport. It was the first time anything had happened to give them any action, and they were all excited. They ran all the way to the hangar, and Larry shouted orders for the mechanics to run the plane on the field while he and Jim donned helmets and goggles and leather coats.

A red autogiro *Red Bird II*, which had succeeded the *Red Bird*, the plane that last year had crashed in a forest and been smashed beyond hope of repair, was wheeled out into the open, and the two young men climbed aboard. With a roar the engine started and the plane began to move across the ground. It rose gently into the air, and after circling once over the airport Larry headed toward the south. It passed to the right of the college buildings and roared over highways that stretched like white ribbons on the face of the earth. Automobiles looked like bugs crawling along, and people were no larger than tiny ants. The sun gleamed brightly on the huge paddles as they spun around, cutting through the air and sending the plane through the sky at an ever increasing rate of speed.

CHAPTER VI

Foiled

AFTER SEVERAL MINUTES of flying, the young men
began to watch the ground below them carefully.
If the gypsies were camped within five miles of
Vernon, they would soon come upon the camp.

Larry turned in his seat and pointed downward.
At first Jim did not understand. They were flying
over a highway, and Larry was driving the plane at
a terrific rate. Two automobiles were parked, one
behind the other, and men were standing about.
Then Jim knew what Larry had meant. Most of
the men on the road wore blue coats, and their silver buttons gleamed in the sun. They were Inspector Dugan and his men. Evidently one of the cars
had suffered a flat tire, and the men were repairing
it before they could proceed. At this rate, Jim and
Larry would arrive at the gypsy camp before the
authorities. So much the better. If policemen went

barging into the gypsy camp, the gypsies might become alarmed and suspicious, and if Beverly were with them they might hide her. As it was, they might receive Jim and Larry pleasantly, if the latter pretended to be only two aviators in distress.

Larry zoomed his plane low over the distressed policemen and waved gayly as the men stared upward. The men were unresponding, so Larry continued on his way. They flew over more roads and houses and fields. They flew low over a thick growth of trees, a miniature forest standing against the side of a mountain. A thin spiral of smoke curled its way upward from a small opening in the trees, and Larry pointed to it, gesticulating excitedly. Jim nodded. Around the fire, from which the smoke could be seen curling, were standing three or four wagons, and moving figures flitted back and forth between the trees. The gypsy camp!

The young aviator circled round, searching for a suitable landing place for his plane. Lucky he had an autogiro, it was able to land and take off in a much smaller runway than another type of airship. There was scarcely any place to land here. Both sides of the road were heavily wooded, and if he flew on to where there was a field, they would have to walk back quite a distance to the gypsy camp site. Larry decided to take a chance and land in the road. It was a road not much used but in good condition. There were no vehicles in sight, so he nosed his ship downward.

The autogiro bumped to a landing, rolled a few feet, and stopped. Immediately Larry and Jim jumped out.

"Let's try strategy with these fellows," Larry said hastily. "We will pretend there is something wrong with the plane and we had to land to fix it. If we throw them completely off their guard, we might learn something."

"Righto!" Jim agreed tensely. "Get busy," he added in a low tone, stripping off his goggles. "There is a man watching us from the woods on the other side of the road."

"Yes," Larry said in a louder voice, especially for the benefit of the listener, "it was a lucky thing for us that this road was here. The motor is spluttering pretty badly."

Larry bent attentively over the engine, and Jim hung over his shoulder, offering suggestions. Not by a word or sign did they show that they were aware of being observed. Larry gave Jim an oily rag, and both of them were busily engaged in doing nothing much when the watcher decided to make himself known. He left the clump of trees and advanced toward the autogiro.

Larry looked up, perfect simulation of surprise on his face.

"Hullo," he said pleasantly.

The man nodded but did not speak. He was not a pleasant-looking individual. His clothes were dusty and wrinkled. Beneath his short jacket could be seen a red sash bound about his waist. His skin was dark, and his eyes black and piercing. Undoubtedly he was one of the gypsies. He swaggered forward nonchalantly and stood watching both men and the plane.

"Can you tell us where we are?" Larry asked again. "We were forced to land to repair the engine, but we don't know where we are."

"That is unfortunate," the man said in a deep, guttural voice. "Is the damage severe?"

"No," Larry continued conversationally. "It won't take long to fix it ship-shape."

The two young men bent attentively over the engine, and the gypsy edged closer. He appeared fascinated by the mechanism of the giant bird. Larry and Jim had apparently forgotten his very existence, until he tapped Larry on the shoulder.

"Is it difficult to fly?" he asked.

The young men exchanged glances.

"Do you mean to learn to operate a plane, or as a passenger?" Larry asked.

"As—a passenger," the man answered.

"No," Larry laughed. "It is thrilling. Get in, I think the engine is O. K. now. I'll take you for a spin."

Here was an opportunity to establish a friendship between a gypsy and himself. If he won the man's confidence, he might learn something about Beverly.

Larry and the gypsy climbed into the cockpits and Jim stood by the side of the road and watched them take off. The plane circled overhead and flew straight into the north. For several minutes Larry gave the gypsy the most thrilling experience in his life. When he finally set the plane down again in the road, the gypsy was beaming with delight. He shook hands profusely with Larry and Jim.

"Gosh, Larry, I'm thirsty," Jim said obviously hinting.

"My camp is just beyond the trees," the gypsy volunteered. "If you will honor us, I shall be most glad to offer you clear, cool spring water."

"We accept with many thanks," Larry said promptly, jumping from the plane. He had begun to think his ruse to win the gypsy's friendship wouldn't amount to much.

The man led the way from the road to his camp. Women and children were sunning themselves in the clearing where the setting sun shone down. The men gathered there looked suspiciously at Larry and Jim as they entered the camp. One or two approached the young men's guide with dark glances and angry words. He replied to them in a language neither young man could understand, and gesticulated beamingly toward the road and then up at the sky.

"Telling them about the ride," Larry murmured to Jim.

Several other gypsies, after a brief conversation with their guide, departed through the trees.

"I hope they keep their hands off the controls," Larry said in a worried undertone. "I don't mind their looking at the ship, but I don't want them fooling with it."

"I don't think they will," Jim replied laughing. "Most of them will be too scared to get familiar with it."

"Keep your eyes open for Bev," Larry said under his breath as their guide turned to them.

"If the gentlemen will be seated by the camp fire, I will bring them something with which to refresh themselves."

He departed, and the young men looked about at the wagons with interest. Most of the wagons had the doors at the back open, and the windows swung wide to let in the air and sunlight. But there was one wagon, standing apart from the rest, that was shut up tight. As they watched, two men approached the wagon. One entered, the other sat down on the steps and puffed reflectively on a pipe. After a while the first man came out and sat down beside the other man. Was the wagon empty, or did it house a secret that the two men were prepared to guard? They were most protective in their attitude.

Their guide came back, carrying a tin pitcher of cool spring water. The young men refreshed themselves and conversed pleasantly with the gypsy.

"The wagons look cheerful," Larry commented. "It must be great to travel about like that, doing nothing all day."

"What is in that wagon over there?" Jim asked pointing to the wagon which the two gypsy men were obviously guarding.

"My grandmother is very sick," the gypsy said, his voice sad. "We are obliged to keep her in darkness for a time."

"Indeed?" Larry asked.

"Yes, it is most unfortunate. Perhaps the gods will be kind and restore her to health soon."

At that moment an uproar arose beyond the camp, and all the gypsies bristled to attention. The

young men could easily guess what it was. Inspector
Dugan and his men had arrived. The policemen
had several men in their clutches as they approached the camp, and these they propelled
roughly over the uneven ground. Larry and Jim
flashed warning glances at the inspector, plainly
telling him not to recognize them.

"Who is the leader of this bunch?" Inspector
Dugan roared, evidently trying to strike terror to
the hearts of the gypsies by his rough tones.

"I am the leader." A tall, swarthy man stepped
forward from one of the wagons.

"I have a warrant to search your camp," the inspector said. "Get busy, boys," he told his men.
"Search everything in sight."

The gypsies threw dark glances at the bluecoats
as the men tramped through the wagons, but they
made no effort to stop them until they came to the
wagon that was set a little apart from the others.
Then the gypsy that had ridden in the plane with
Larry stepped forward and pleaded with the inspector not to disturb his sick grandmother. The
inspector was adamant. He had to search every
wagon in the camp. At last the gypsies yielded, on
the condition that they might enter first and pre-
pare the old woman for the disturbance of the
policemen. Two gypsies entered and were inside for

a few moments before one appeared and beckoned to the inspector. The inspector stepped forward and went into the wagon. He was inside but a moment.

"Nothing there," he said when he reappeared.

The inspector and his men and Larry and Jim were disappointed. The gypsy camp had been searched from end to end, and nothing had been discovered. They had been so sure that Beverly was here. They had not even discovered a clue to her whereabouts. If she were not with the gypsies, where was she? Nothing that had been stolen from the art shop in Vernon was uncovered in the camp, so the inspector could not arrest anyone. The owner of the art shop had been unable to give an accurate description of the man who robbed him, making it difficult for the inspector to accuse anyone of the crime. But it was not the robbery that was worrying the men from Vernon. It was Beverly. Where could she be, if she was not here with the gypsies?

The inspector and his men reluctantly climbed back into their autos and drove off. They were despondent. The search on which they had started out so eagerly had ended in failure. Where were they to begin a new search now? All indications had pointed to Beverly's presence with the gypsies, and yet a close search had revealed nothing.

With heavy hearts Larry and Jim watched the police drive off. All hopes of finding Beverly here had fled. They were anxious now only to leave the gypsies as far behind as possible. There was no use wasting any more time here. Their mission was complete, and had failed. They would have to go back to Vernon and pick up Beverly's trail anew. But from where? They had no clues whatever to work on.

"The police," the gypsy was muttering, "are blundering fools! Suspicious of gypsies! Always accusing gypsies of theft and crime!"

"What did they want?" Jim asked, leading the gypsy on to talk.

"Looking for a girl. A white girl." The gypsy laughed. "Search the gypsy camp! They found nothing. Perhaps now they will rest quietly. They could find nothing if it was under their noses!"

"Well, we've got to be going," Larry said.

The gypsy accompanied them back to the auto-giro and watched them climb into the cockpits. The young men waved to him as the plane soared away overhead. Larry headed the plane back to Vernon. The sun was setting, and twilight was settling down over the world when they landed at the airport. Together they walked to their hotel in Vernon. Both were silent, thoughtful, and depressed. They ate their dinner in the hotel dining room and then went into the lounge.

"Shall we telephone the girls at Vernon now?" Jim asked finally.

"We might as well," Larry said, sighing. "There is no use putting it off any longer. I hate to think of telling them," he said. "They counted so much on having good news."

"So did we," Jim smiled ruefully. "This thing has me stumped."

"And me," Larry acknowledged. "In the Secret Service I'm used to tracking down smugglers and murderers, but I can't find Beverly. I've traced thieves on scarcely any clues at all, and now I'm stumped on this."

"I wonder if there was anything in that wagon which the inspector insisted on searching," Jim mused.

"Yes, I've wondered the same thing. The story of the sick grandmother sounded funny to me," Larry admitted.

"I suppose if there had been anything the inspector would have said something," Jim continued.

"That's so," Larry said. He rose slowly. "Come along, we might as well telephone the Alphas."

The two young men proceeded to a telephone booth and before long had Shirley on the other end of the wire. They could tell by the suppressed eagerness in her voice that the girls were all longing for the news. Larry did the talking and he told her everything that had happened. None of his own disappointment was in his voice. He kept his tone light and cheerful as possible, even joking a little about the gypsy who had ridden in the plane with him.

Shirley listened silently. Her voice, when she spoke finally, sounded choked and unsteady. Tears were very near the surface, and Larry did not keep her at the telephone long. He knew she wanted to get away by herself, so he said good-bye and turned back to Jim.

"Gosh, I feel like a cad," he said uneasily. "I hated like the deuce to give her the bad news."

A bell boy approached Jim and handed him a telegram which had just arrived. The two young men sat down on the divan in the lounge, and Jim read the yellow slip of paper. When he had finished, he laughed shortly and sat staring at the printed lines.

"What is it?" Larry asked. "Bad news?"

"No," Jim answered slowly. "No, I suppose you would call it good news. It means that the position as engineer which I have been trying all summer to get is at last open to me."

"Fine!" Larry said.

"Yes," Jim nodded slowly, "it is fine. A chance of a lifetime, and I don't know whether to take it or not."

"Why on earth shouldn't you?" Larry gasped.

"They want me to leave within three weeks," Jim answered. "Right now, with Beverly missing and all, I don't feel like traveling away out to Wyoming."

Larry sat silent for several minutes. At last he spoke, and his voice was gently persuading. "You better take it, Jim. There is nothing you can do here, and this job means a lot to your future. Beverly wouldn't want to deprive you of your big chance."

"No, she wouldn't," Jim admitted.

"If you throw it up," Larry continued, "she will feel that she is to blame, if she ever hears of it. That would make her feel badly—you know it."

Jim folded the telegram carefully and put it in his pocket. "I suppose you are right," he said at last. "We have three weeks, Larry, in which to find Beverly. At the end of that time, whether she is found—or not, I take a train to Wyoming."

CHAPTER VII

A Letter

SHIRLEY turned away from the telephone and made her way blindly up to her room. It had not been good news that Larry had given her. They were just where they had been days ago—before they had discovered the gypsies' hiding place. Indeed, now they were totally at a loss. Before there had been a glimmer of hope—that the gypsies would have Beverly. Then they looked day after day for some word to come of the gypsies, but now they had nothing to base even a faint hope on.

The other Alphas were waiting in her room for her. When she entered they could tell at once by the dejected look on her face that she had not had good news. They had started up with expectation, but now they sank back slowly into their former positions.

"Let's have the bad news," Lenora said wearily.

Shirley told them what Larry had told her. The girls greeted the account with woeful silence. Each one of them was keenly disappointed. Lois and Lenora stared moodily out the window. Anne and Rosalie idly turned the pages of a magazine, striving to keep calm and hide how hurt they really were. Shirley, however, gave full vent to her feelings. She flung herself across her bed, and broken sobs were smothered in the pillows. The other girls looked from one to the other with frightened eyes. They knew Shirley missed Beverly, but they had never guessed that she really felt as badly as this. During the days they had lived in suspense, Shirley had gone about calm and quiet, giving no hint of the tumult within her. This final blow had been too much.

The other girls gathered about the bed and attempted to quiet Shirley, but heartrending sobs tore their way to the surface. Lois slipped an unobtrusive handkerchief into Shirley's hand, while Anne patted her shoulder consolingly.

"Buck up, old girl," Lenora said kindly. "It won't do any good to cry."

"B-but it m-makes me f-feel b-better," Shirley gulped.

"You will have me doing it," Rosalie said, sniffing tremulously.

"Don't," Lois begged. "One at a time, please! If anybody else wants to cry, wait a while."

"I'm sorry I was such a baby," Shirley said, sitting up at length and endeavoring to wipe away the tears, "but I couldn't hold in any longer."

"I suggest that we have a crying bee," Lenora said practically. "It will help us all to get the blues out of our system."

At the suggestion a slow smile broke through Shirley's tears. "Silly," she said. "We would look cute, wouldn't we?"

Gradually the girls helped Shirley to restore her self-control, and they talked on cheerfully of many things. They could even discuss Beverly without breaking down.

"You know," Lenora said, "plans are being made to produce *Hamlet* after the Christmas holidays."

"By the junior class?" asked Lois.

"Yes. You will all remember in our freshman year we produced *Romeo and Juliet*. It was such a success that now we have decided to give *Hamlet*," Lenora explained.

"With the same cast?" Anne wanted to know.

"Lenora has been chosen as stage director again," volunteered Rosalie.

"That means more headaches for me," sighed

Lenora. "I want Shirley to play Hamlet and Lois to play Ophelia."

"Whoops, my dear!" Lois giggled. "Fancy me in the costume of Ophelia!"

"This will be good," prophesied Shirley. "With Lois as Ophelia and me as Hamlet, it will be a riot!"

Anne laughed at the prospect. "Be sure you don't turn the play into a comedy."

"You better play it seriously and not try any tricks," Lenora warned, "or I'll jump on you."

The girls trooped down to dinner, discussing the play. It gave them something new to talk about, and they were thankful. For a few minutes at least they could forget the awful anxiety about Beverly.

Three more days passed, and no news reached the people in Vernon. They began seriously to doubt whether they ever would hear anything. Jim and Larry, together with Inspector Dugan, had exhausted every possibility. They were at a standstill. They knew no way to turn.

Life at the college went on much as it would have done had Beverly been present. Classes formed and dispersed day after day, studies were worried and talked over, girls entered sports and after-school activities, and much of the excitement that had attended Beverly's disappearance died down.

Then one afternoon Shirley was in her room

studying the latest literature lesson when Lenora entered with the mail.

"Hi, there, Hamlet, some letters for you."

"Good." Shirley tossed her book to one side and grabbed the envelopes Lenora held out to her. She glanced at the postmarks one by one. "Two from home," she said idly. Then she looked up in surprise. "Hullo, here is one from Pennsylvania," she said. "I wonder who that is from?"

"You might open it," suggested Lenora, undisguised curiosity in her voice.

Shirley laughed. "That's true. I guess that would be the best course." She tore the flap open and lifted out the folded sheets.

"They had a lot to say, whoever it is," Lenora commented, noting the thickly scrawled pages and the number of them.

Shirley turned over the pages until she came to the last one. "It's from Gerry Foster," she said in pleased surprise.

Gerry Foster had graduated from Vernon last June. During the Alphas' freshman year they had become great friends with Gerry, and it did not seem so very strange that she should now write to Shirley.

"Well, well." Lenora deposited herself cross-legged beside Shirley on the bed. "What does the dear girl have to say?"

"She sends you all her regards," Shirley murmured, her eyes glancing over the pages.

"Considerate of her," Lenora drawled. "I remember the trick we played on her when we were freshmen," she continued musingly. "Was she burned up when she——"

Shirley, who had been reading her letter and not paying the slightest attention to Lenora's inconsequential ramblings, grasped her friend's arm tightly and gave it a shake.

"Lenora! Lenora!"

"Well?" Lenora gasped. "What's the matter? You haven't seen a ghost, have you?" that young lady demanded at Shirley's excited cries.

"It's Gerry! She—she has seen Beverly!"

Lenora nearly fell off the bed in her amazement. "She—she has what?" she almost shouted.

"Yes. Listen, this is what Gerry says: 'You know I am staying with my aunt in this little town in Pennsylvania, and big events are few and far between. Two days ago the County Fair opened. That has stirred up some excitement in the neighborhood. Yesterday I went to the Fair, the first one I ever attended. There were side shows, you know the kind, with the sword swallowers and fire eaters.

I was standing before one tent, looking at the grotesquely drawn pictures, when I spied a young man and woman standing across the midway. As sure as I live, I am sure that the girl was Beverly. I had read about her disappearance in the papers, and that made me doubly anxious to make sure. The girl I saw must have felt me looking at her, for she looked up suddenly and met my gaze. She recognized me, I am sure. Indeed, she even smiled a trifle. Then she gave one glance at the young man with her, and they both turned away. I was across the road in two shakes of a lamb's tail, but when I got to where they had been standing, they had disappeared.

" 'I haven't told this experience to anyone, because now I am uncertain whether the girl actually was Beverly. If it had been, surely Beverly would have stopped and talked with me? If it was not Beverly, then it was her double. She was as tall as Beverly, had the same curly brown hair, and her smile was the same funny impulsive one. The man with her was young, deeply tanned, as was the girl, and handsome. He reminded me of a gypsy, with his black hair and bright eyes.' "

Shirley finished reading and looked up at Lenora, her cheeks flushed and eyes bright.

"Well, I'll be——" Lenora said gaspingly. "Come

on." She rose to her feet and dragged Shirley **up** with her. "We've got to spread this news around. I know some folks that will be surprised."

"You tell the girls," Shirley said breathlessly. "I'm off to Vernon to tell Jim and Larry and Inspector Dugan."

"Righto!" Lenora called gayly.

Shirley, flying madly down the stairs, collided with Lois and Anne.

"Where in the world are you going at that express train speed?" Lois demanded.

"Yes, what is all the excitement?" Anne wanted to know.

"Ask Lenora," Shirley flung over her shoulder. "We've had big news."

Those last words sent the two Alpha members scurrying up the stairs in search of Lenora.

Shirley fled out of the Hall and down College Avenue into Vernon. She burst into Inspector Dugan's office, breathlessly interrupting his conference with Jim and Larry. The three men stood silent and amazed as Shirley read them the important portion of Gerry's letter.

"Yypee!" Larry flung his hat into the air. "That is the first good news we've had in weeks!"

"It sure is," Jim agreed. "Where is this fair being held?"

"It rather looks as if it might be the gypsies after all," Inspector Dugan said slowly.

"It also looks as though they aren't keeping her much of a prisoner, if they let her be seen openly at a fair," Shirley commented.

That set a new train of thought buzzing in their minds. It looked almost as if Beverly were absenting herself willingly. If she were free enough to appear at a county fair, she was surely free enough to send them a message to quell their fears. What could they make of it? She had been with a young man. Who was he? Why was she with him? The four could offer no explanation.

"We'll hop off at once in the *Red Bird*," Larry proposed. "We ought to arrive at the Fair tonight."

CHAPTER VIII

Robbery

LET US, NOW, go back to the night when Beverly left Chadwick Hall to mail her letters. She lingered for a few moments on the porch of the building, gazing up at the sky. The clouds were lowering, and they were sure to have rain before the night was over. She had to go to Vernon to get stamps for her letters, and she might be caught in the storm. Should she wait until tomorrow? She stepped down off the porch with a shrug. A little wetting wouldn't hurt her; besides, she would hurry and probably be back before the storm broke.

She walked briskly toward Vernon, giving herself no time for leisurely dreaming. But her thoughts raced over what the gypsy had said earlier in the evening. Of course she didn't for one moment believe what the woman prophesied, yet it wasn't exactly cheering to think that something

unpleasant might be going to happen in the near
future. Common sense told her that no one had
the power to look into the future and see what was
coming, whether good or bad. But, she reminded
herself, there had been times when gypsies' prophe-
cies had come true. Anyway, regardless of what the
gypsy had said, she wouldn't let it worry her.

It was a warm night, and she never had enjoyed
fast walking, so she slowed her pace. If it rained,
it rained, that was all. She would rather take her
time and enjoy the walk. The night was still, almost uncommonly so. "Silence precedes the storm,"
she reminded herself. The leaves on the trees stirred,
and it was as if tiny voices were whispering therein.
Occasionally an automobile passed, its headlights
cutting through the darkness like a knife. The
homes along the way were lighted pleasantly, coz-
ily. Beverly always liked lighted windows; they
stirred her imagination. She could imagine the people who lived in the homes by the lights that shone
out into the world. A lot of lamps, dispelling the
darkness of the houses with their friendly bright-
ness, meant cheerful, happy people. Dark houses,
with only a dim, single light, probably meant
stingy, unfriendly persons trying to save on elec-
tricity.

She crossed the street and stopped before an art

shop. She stood gazing at the display in the window for several minutes. There was a pair of book
ends, carved into the form of white elephants.
They would look fine on her desk, and she had always wanted a pair of book ends. White elephants,
too, were supposed to be lucky. There was also a
desk set there. She really needed a desk set more
than she did book ends.

"To buy or not to buy," she musingly misquoted
Hamlet.

From the desk set her gaze traveled back to the
book ends. She didn't need them, but she wanted
them. It was so much nicer to buy something one
wanted than something one needed. Her eye spied
then a talisman of Chinese jade. That would be
nice. There was, too, a picture of a giant sailboat
breasting white-capped waves on an ocean of deep-
est blue. She would love to have that to hang over
her desk, but the room was now too full of pictures. Shirley had a hobby of picking up a picture
the minute she espied one she liked and tacking it
up on the wall. If Beverly, too, acquired the habit,
the walls would be covered with pictures. There
was a delicate china chocolate set that would be
just the thing for the Alpha meetings. Should she
buy it?

She had come down here to get postage stamps,

and here she was debating about things she had
never thought of until this minute. A man strolled
down the street and stopped beside her to look in
the window. Beverly gave him merely a fleeting
glance. Her eyes were fastened on the white ele-
phant book ends. She had decided to buy those.

She turned and entered the shop. She had to wait
several minutes before the shopkeeper appeared
from the room beyond the store. He was a thin,
elderly man, extremely nervous and excitable. She
told him what she wanted, and he turned to take
the white elephants out of the window, chattering
all the while. He had had a great many sales of
these book ends in the last few weeks. He had had
twenty-five pairs of them, and now this was the
last one. It was really a lucky thing that she had
waited no longer to purchase them, for he was sure
he could get no more. While he was chattering to
her and wrapping up the book ends into a nice neat
parcel, the bell over the door tinkled, and the man
who had stopped beside Beverly strode in.

In the mellow light of the shop he was dark and
swarthy. Beverly decided he must be a gypsy, but
the gypsies were supposed to have left town hours
ago. His right hand was in his coat pocket, and he
pushed it forward insinuatingly, at the same time
rasping out a brisk command to the shopkeeper to

put his hands above his head. It was a robbery, and a desperate one. The man grasped the money in the cash register, which wasn't much, and turned to go.

The shopkeeper was whimpering and wailing. Beverly almost smiled despite the seriousness of the situation. The shop owner was almost comical in his distress. Instead of doing something to prevent the robbery, he was merely wailing like a child.

The gypsy paused in his flight to the door and his eyes fastened on the watch on Beverly's wrist. The tiny timepiece was expensive, and he recognized that fact. He could get much money for that piece of jewelry. He came close to Beverly, and before the girl was aware of his intention he had grasped her wrist and torn the watch from her arm. Then he dashed out into the night.

That final act of his aroused Beverly as nothing else could have done. She prized her wrist watch beyond anything else that she possessed. It had been given to her when she rescued Shirley from the Hall fire, and nothing should make her part with it.

"Telephone the police," she shouted over her shoulder to the terrified, hysterical shopkeeper and dashed out after the gypsy.

She had some wild idea of stopping the bandit

and making him return her watch, and she did not
realize how foolish her impulsive chase was. On the
pavement she stopped and glanced around. There
he was! The man was just disappearing around the
corner at the end of the street. Beverly bounded
after him. She was extremely light and active on
her feet, and it did not take her long to cover the
few paces to the corner. The man was running in
the shadows ahead of her. The street, here, was
poorly lighted and heavily bordered with trees. It
might be very easy to lose sight of the thief. This
thought sent her sprinting forward with more
speed.

The man loomed up ahead of her, and Beverly
flung herself on him, grasping his arm. "Give me
that watch!" she commanded.

He endeavored to shake loose her hold and flee,
but Beverly hung on grimly. She was fighting for
her precious wrist watch, and then, too, she might
be able to make the man return the money he had
stolen from the art shop. Surely the police would
give chase in a few minutes! The man struggled
fiercely to loosen her grip, and Beverly felt her hold
slipping. He was too agile and strong for her to
keep a firm grip on him. There was a way to summon help! She opened her mouth and let out a
piercing scream. Surely that would bring some-

body! She opened her lips to emit another shout, but a dirty hand closed over her mouth. The man did not want the townspeople, and especially the police, rushing to the scene.

The positions were now reversed. The man was struggling to retain his hold of Beverly, and the girl was fighting with all her strength to break his hold. She was lithe and strongly athletic, but she could not free herself. His arm closed down, pinioning her arms to her sides. Bodily he lifted her and carried her from the street through the bushes on one side. Beverly saw something large loom up out of the darkness, and the man mounted several steps. He tapped lightly with his foot, and a door was opened. He set Beverly down on the inside and pushed her none too gently onto a bunk in the corner.

CHAPTER IX

Captive

FOR A MOMENT Beverly lay still, too stunned to move. The inside of this house, or whatever it was, was not large. It was about seven feet wide and twelve feet long. A small table stood in the middle, and, besides several box-stools and the bunk on which she lay, it was the only furnishing in the room. A candle standing on the table threw into bold relief the two figures that stood glowering at her.

The man who had brought her here had flung his cap to one side and was frowning at her. The other, a woman, old and wrinkled, cackled in amused laughter. With a shock Beverly recognized the same gypsy that had told her fortune earlier in the evening. It was then that she knew she was in a wagon, one of the gypsy wagons, and at that very moment it started moving.

She jumped to her feet and stormily confronted the man.

"Let me out of here—at once!" Her voice was trembling with anger.

A gleam of admiration sprang into the man's eyes, hiding the anger that had been there a moment ago. The gypsy woman laughed shrilly.

"Dimiti, the lady wants to leave us!"

The man smiled cruelly. "If she had not run after me she would not be here. You are very foolish, my little one," he said to Beverly. "Why did you try to stop me?"

"You committed robbery," Beverly said bluntly.

"True," he acknowledged, "but you could not stop me."

"You must let me go," Beverly insisted.

The man shook his head. "You would immediately set the police on the trail of the poor gypsies."

"She is very beautiful, no?" the woman cackled. "She might bring us much gold, Dimiti."

"It was that of which I was thinking," the man nodded.

"You mean—you are going to hold me—for ransom?" Beverly gasped.

The man shrugged his shoulders. "The money is not important to me."

"But it is to the rest of us," the woman interrupted. "It would be well, Dimiti, to keep the girl here."

The man nodded. "She can have this wagon."

"You wouldn't dare keep me here," Beverly said, forcing confidence into her voice.

The wagon had stopped again, and now the man and the woman moved towards the door. The woman carried the candle with her, and above the yellow flame shadows danced over her face, making it appear more dark and evil than before. Beverly looked from her to the man. His face was set in a cruel smile. She did not like the light in his eyes. It made her afraid, but not for the world would she show her fear to these two.

The man and woman went out, closing the door behind them and leaving her in total darkness. She flung herself at the door, but it was locked. She was a captive of the gypsies. She was a prisoner here in this dark, dirty wagon of the gypsies. She felt her way to the bunk in the corner and crouched there. The memory of the evil faces of the gypsies came to her, and she shivered. Why, oh, why had she been so impulsive and followed that man! She had followed him to get her wrist watch back, and now she did not have the watch anyway, and in the bargain she had let herself into something worse than robbery. They wouldn't dare hold her or harm her, she told herself. The thought of the old woman and the man as she had last seen them came to her. Their finality had been conclusive. They meant to hold her prisoner, of that there was no doubt.

She sank back dejectedly against the wall. Her impulsiveness always led her into difficulties. Why would she do rash things without thinking? If only she had not followed the gypsy but stayed and told the police. They would, eventually, have gotten her watch back for her. Now she did not have the watch, and she herself was in a dangerous position.

What were they doing now? Probably dividing the money stolen from the art shop. She had hoped no one would come here to her wagon. She especially wanted to avoid Dimiti. She had not liked the light in his eyes when he looked at her. He would be utterly ruthless, she knew. Even the thought of the old woman set her trembling. What was she going to do? She beat impotent fists on the bunk at her sides. She wouldn't remain a prisoner! She wouldn't calmly accept the fact that she was a captive! She would fight for her freedom! But what good would it do? There were a great number of them, and she was alone. She was utterly friendless here in the midst of a tribe of gypsies.

The wagon began to move again, and still she

remained alone. No one came to her, and for that she was thankful. Gradually she sank down on the bunk until she was lying flat on her back, staring up at the black ceiling. Her thoughts raced fearfully over the possibilities of what might happen to her here. But gradually she became drowsy. She had been in the open air much that day, and she was tired. She relaxed, and despite the seriousness of her position, she slept.

When the wagon rumbled to a halt she awoke, startled. She had forgotten for a while where she was. The wagon was still dark, but not as dark as it had been the night before. She sat up and stretched her cramped muscles. She felt refreshed and—hungry. It struck her as slightly incongruous that even in the most desperate straits she could still be hungry. A slight slit of gray light showed above her bunk. Her exploring fingers found the catch and swung the window wide. The opening was large, but not large enough for her to climb through. Escape had been her first thought, but it was impossible. Rain drifted in to her, and she half closed the shutters again. At least she would have air in here.

She peered out, seeking for a glimpse of her captors, but no one was in sight. She could hear voices, though, and they seemed to be coming toward her

wagon. She offered up a quick prayer that it was
not Dimiti and the old woman she had seen last
night. The door was opened, and the same two entered. Her prayers had not been answered. She
stood and faced them, defiantly silent.

The old woman set a bowl down on the table. A
mysterious brown substance spilled over the edge.
What was that for? Beverly wondered. The man
stood in the doorway and grinned at her. The old
hag dipped her fingers into the bowl and advanced
toward Beverly. She caught Beverly's arm and applied her wet fingers thereto. Beverly pulled away
quickly. The woman's fingers had left a dark stain
on Beverly's white skin.

"You have mixed it well, Orlenda," the man
commended. "You see," he explained to Beverly,
"since you are to be our guest for a time, it is well
that we should—disguise you. The liquid is to make
your skin darker so, if anyone should see you, you
could pass for one of us."

They were going to stain her skin dark like
theirs! Beverly fumed inwardly. They shouldn't
touch her! With one movement she sent the table
crashing against the wall. Orlenda, with a wild cry,
sprang to retrieve the precious bowl of liquid. The
man sprang forward after Beverly. The girl eluded
him and ran for the door. She grasped hold of the

door jamb with both hands and screamed loudly as the man tried to draw her back into the wagon. His hand closed over her mouth to stop the screaming, while the other arm encircled her waist. She felt her hold slipping and redoubled her efforts to free herself. But it was useless. The man was strong, much stronger than she. He drew her back into the interior of the wagon and with his two hands pinned her arms to her sides.

"Now, you she-cat," he gritted between clenched teeth, "scream all you want. There is no one within miles to hear you."

If no one could hear her, what was the use of screaming? Beverly stood silent in his grasp, her breast heaving and her breath coming in gasps. The old woman sidled toward her and suddenly struck her across the face. The blow hurt, it brought the tears to Beverly's eyes, but the girl stood silently scornful. The man spoke sharply to Orlenda, and the woman brought the bowl forward. Not all of the liquid had been spilled. There was enough left to accomplish her purpose.

Beverly's spirit shrank away every time the claw-like hand of the gypsy woman touched her. She wanted to flee from this horrible old creature, but the man's grasp was firm on her arms. Fighting was of no avail, so she might just as well submit in graceful if stormy silence. The old woman applied the liquid generously to Beverly's face and neck and arms. When she had finished she laughed in evident delight.

"Look, Dimiti, does she not make a beautiful gypsy?"

The man released his hold and pushed Beverly toward the bunk. "Ah," he answered the old woman, "she is indeed bewitching. If you could teach her to read the cards, Orlenda, she would make much money for us. All the young men like to have their fortunes read by a pretty gypsy."

Beverly said not a word, but she made up her mind nothing would make her enter the practices of the gypsies. Never would she tell fortunes to earn money for them! She watched in silence as the two conversed in a tongue unintelligible to her. What were they plotting now? Finally they turned and left the wagon, carefully locking the door behind them. She was to be left in peace—for how long? She looked down at her arms. The skin was as dark now as any of the gypsies'. How long would the stain remain? she wondered. Would it wash off? She stood up and thrust her hand out the window. For a long while she held it there in the rain, but when she finally drew it in none of the brown stain had been washed off. No doubt it would have to wear off!

Footsteps were approaching the wagon again, and she sank down on the bunk. The door was opened, and a woman entered. Beverly had never seen her before. The woman set down a tray on which was a steaming cup of hot coffee and something in a dish that sent up a delicious aroma. Beverly made no motion toward the food until the woman had left. Then gingerly she tasted the concoction in the tin dish. It was good, whatever it was. She ate the food, but the coffee was brewed too strongly to suit her, so she let it set. She went back to the window and stared out at the rain. It was a dismal day. The woman returned for the dishes and without a word withdrew again. Evidently they did not mean to trouble her.

She stood at her post by the window when the wagon began to move again. The trees and bushes passed slowly. Minute by minute and hour by hour she was being taken farther and farther away from her friends at Vernon. What were they thinking? Would Shirley worry when she didn't appear at their room all through the night? Of course she would! She worried when Beverly was even five minutes late to keep an appointment with her. What would people think? Would they guess that the gypsies had kinaped her? Surely the owner of the art shop would tell them she had run after the gypsy, and from that they could guess the rest. The owner of the art shop was such a funny old gentleman, he might even forget that the man was a gypsy!

The words of the gypsy's prophecy came uppermost in her mind. Orlenda had said a dark period would come into her life. She would be in danger, and it would cause much worry to her friends. Was this what she had meant?

CHAPTER X

Anselo

THE DAYS PASSED with aggravating slowness. Minutes dragged into hours, and hours into days. Beverly remained shut up in her prison all the time. At times she paced the narrow space for endless hours. She felt that if something didn't happen soon she would go mad. This solitude was nerve racking. The woman who brought her meals never said a word. She came and went in absolute silence. Neither Dimiti nor Orlenda had been near the wagon, and for that she was thankful. She wanted something to happen, but she didn't care to have a visit from those two.

The wagons had been stopped since early morning. Beverly had spent most of the day at the window, gazing out at the sky and the earth. She could never get a glimpse of the other gypsies. They kept her wagon turned so that the window opened away

from the camp. She could not have said how many
there were in the band. The sun was setting in the
west, and a rosy glow was over the landscape. Beverly leant her head wearily against the window
casement and sighed. By now her friends back in
Vernon would be worried sick. Her parents, too,
how they would worry!

There was a sudden scratching noise on the
wagon beneath the window and a ball of fur came
hurtling in toward her. The fur developed into the
form of a little monkey, who threw himself on her
and clung tightly with his fuzzy arms about her
neck. For a moment she was too surprised to do
anything, and then she tried gently to remove his
hold. He chattered excitedly in her ear and whimpered beseechingly. He was frightened, the poor
little thing. He pressed his fuzzy face to hers, chattering all the while.

"What's the matter, boy?" she murmured sooth-
ingly. How on earth did one talk to monkeys?

"Cheeko! Cheeko!" a laughing, masculine voice
drifted in to her.

The monkey in her arms trembled at the sound
of the voice.

"Your master is coming, Cheeko, if that is your
name," she whispered.

"There you are, you little rascal!" A sleek, dark

head of a young man appeared on the outside of the window. "Come here!" He endeavored to get his hands on the monkey, but the monkey leaped from Beverly's arms to the table and crouched there.

"He knows you are going to whip him," Beverly said wisely.

"I'm not going to whip him," the man contradicted, "but the little rascal has my ring."

Beverly noticed then that in one tiny paw the monkey clasped a small band of glittering gold.

"Cheeko, come here!" the man called again but the monkey made no effort to obey. When Beverly moved toward him he eluded her.

"You will have to bribe him," Beverly laughed.

The young man disappeared for a moment. When he returned he held a banana in his hand. "Cheeko, here. Come and get it."

The monkey surveyed his master from his position on the edge of the bunk. His little bead eyes took in the sight of the enticing fruit, and slowly he approached. The fruit was very tempting, and he could not resist. He edged closer until suddenly a long arm swooped in and grasped him. From his master's shoulder, Cheeko regarded Beverly while he devoured the banana.

"He is a cunning little fellow," Beverly laughed.

"But mischievous," the gypsy said, smiling. "He is always getting into trouble and keeps me busy pulling him out of it again. Don't you, Cheeko?"

The monkey looked suitably penitent and nuzzled his master's cheek affectionately. With difficulty the gypsy extracted his ring from the monkey's claw and replaced it on his own finger. The monkey hopped from his master back to Beverly's arms. He snuggled there contentedly.

"He likes you," the gypsy said.

Beverly laughed. "And I like him. Why do you call him Cheeko?"

"When he chatters, it sometimes sounds as though he is saying, 'Cheeko, Cheeko,' so I call him that."

The gypsy fell silent, watching the girl as she played with the monkey. "You are different than when first you came to our camp," he said at last.

Beverly laughed. "How do you mean—different?"

"You are thinner—more grave. Your eyes do not smile like they did at first."

"When did you see me?" Beverly demanded. "I never saw you until just now when you came after Cheeko."

"That is true," the gypsy nodded. "I saw you from a distance. Every day I have watched you from a distance as you stand at your window. You are not happy?"

"Who would be?" Beverly asked. "Shut in this wagon all day is enough to give anyone the jitters. No one to talk to. Nothing to do. It is maddening."

"That is too bad," the gypsy said slowly. "I am sorry I cannot help you. I dare not let you out, but I can come and talk to you when we camp each day. Do you like music?" he asked suddenly. "I am not a great violinist, but I do play."

"When will you play for me?" Beverly asked shyly.

"Tonight, when the moon rises over the trees," he answered.

"What is your name?" Beverly wanted to know.

"Anselo," he answered.

"Why has Dimiti brought me here, and why is he keeping me a prisoner?" Beverly continued.

The gypsy shook his head. "I do not know. Perhaps you can best answer the question of why he brought you here."

"Of course," Beverly said promptly. "To save himself from the police."

"Police?" the young man murmured in surprise. "I have heard nothing of the police. Tell me how it happened he brought you here."

Beverly told him the story of the robbery of the art shop, of her pursuit of Dimiti, and of her being made a prisoner in the wagon.

"You were after your wrist watch, you say?" he mused thoughtfully. "Can you describe it, please?"

"Certainly." Beverly did so, minutely.

"Come, Cheeko," the gypsy said when she had finished. "Good-bye, I will play for you tonight," he added as he turned away.

Beverly decided she liked Anselo and his funny little monkey pet. The young man was refined; he must certainly be well educated. He spoke perfect English, and he had the bearing of a gentleman. There was a world of difference between him and Dimiti.

It was later that night than usual when the woman brought Beverly's supper, and she had scarcely departed with the dirty dishes when the sweet strains of a violin floated in on the night air. Beverly took up her stand at the window and watched Anselo as he approached, playing as he walked. He had kept his word. The moon was just showing over the edge of the trees, silvering the world with its light. Anselo stopped close to the window and continued his playing.

Beverly leant against the window casement and let her thoughts drift with the music. She forgot

her position in the gypsy camp, she forgot her
friends back at Vernon, she even forgot the young
man who was playing. All she heard was the music:
it enchanted her. It seemed to lift her spirits out of
the everyday world into the realms beyond. For a
few moments she walked in a magic world. When
the last quivering notes died away she sighed re-
gretfully.

"That was lovely, superb. You are a genius."

He bowed, smiling. "I am honored that you like
my playing."

"Do play some more," Beverly urged.

"First I will give you something." He put his
hand into the pocket of his jacket and drew forth
something that sparkled in the moonlight. Her
wrist watch! He was giving it back to her. "This
is yours?" he asked.

"Yes, of course. But how did you get it? How
can I thank you?"

He smiled again, and his teeth sparkled like two
fine rows of pearls. "It is enough that you honor
me with your friendship."

Beverly smiled to herself. Gypsies certainly used
flowery language. Did they always compliment
one? How nice the world would be if everyone was
like Anselo—never to hear an unkind word about
oneself, never to meet criticizing stares—but even

then one would tire of always hearing nice things.

Anselo tucked his violin under his chin and drew the bow softly across the strings. He could get more music from a violin than anyone Beverly had ever heard. He should certainly be in a great orchestra, never wasting his talent here in a gypsy camp. She told him this, and he merely laughed and continued to play. He continued with his music, not one piece but many. He played until the moon was high in the heavens and the gypsy camp fire was dying low. Only when he thought that Beverly might be tired did he stop.

"Oh, it was heavenly!" she declared ecstatically. "When will you play for me again?"

"Tomorrow evening?" he asked. "I play every evening when the gypsies gather about the camp fire."

He bowed himself away, and Beverly closed her window for the night. The air was chill, and she was glad to be able to shut out the dampness. She threw herself on her bunk and stared up in the darkness. Today was the first day that she hadn't really hated being shut up here in this wagon. She had made a friend today. She felt her arm where her wrist watch was. How had he persuaded Dimiti to give the watch back to her? She was glad he had, though. The watch meant a lot to her, and she

didn't want to lose it. Had he stolen it from Dimiti?
How ever he had obtained it, it was in her possession now, and Dimiti shouldn't get it again. She
fell asleep and dreamed horrible dreams of the old
woman, Orlenda, and of the man, Dimiti.

CHAPTER XI

Honor Bound

ALL THE NEXT MORNING the gypsy caravan rolled on its way. The roads were uneven, and the wagons jolted from side to side. From her window Beverly could see that the surrounding country was sparsely populated. They passed few houses, and only once did she catch a glimpse of a white person. Thick growth of trees bordered the road. Overhead white clouds sailed slowly in a blanket of blue. The gypsies did not halt for luncheon, and Beverly was beginning to feel uneasy pangs of hunger when at last, late in the afternoon, the wagon halted. She could hear the laughing voices and shouts of the gypsies as they prepared their camp for the night.

The sun was beginning to dip in the west when footsteps approached her wagon. She held her breath. Was it Dimiti? To her surprise, Anselo's smiling face peeped around the door at her. He beckoned her to the doorway.

"Will you walk with me in the woods for a little while?"

Beverly was taken aback with surprise. Was he suggesting that she leave her prison?

"But——"

"It is quite all right. Dimiti has consented," he assured her.

Oh, Dimiti had consented, had he? He considered her his personal property, it seemed. Anger flamed within her, but she wasted no time over words. She stepped out onto the good, firm brown earth. It was wonderful to get her feet on the ground once more. Anselo took her arm and led her away from the gypsy camp. They walked through the trees and the underbrush in silence.

"How did you persuade Dimiti to let me out of the wagon?" she asked at length.

"It is perfectly safe to let you walk here," he answered unconcernedly. "No one is about to see you. I thought you would like it."

"I do like it," she answered quickly. "I hate the thought of that stuffy wagon waiting for me."

"You like the open?" he asked.

"I love it," she answered promptly.

He smiled. "You have the gypsy heart. It is in the gypsy's blood to love the open air; that is why he is restless when he settles down in a city. The gypsy loves to rove, he can never be content in a home of wood and stone."

"Gypsies don't like to work," Beverly said bluntly. "That is why they are so restless. They roam about, living on what the earth produces."

"The things are here in the world for us to use, are they not? Why are they made if no one is meant to use them? The gypsies are not lazy," he defended. "We weave gay baskets and sell them, we mend cooking ware, we——"

"But you couldn't go into an office and work, could you?" she asked laughingly.

He grimaced wryly. "No. The gypsy was not meant to settle into a niche. He needs the wide world for his home."

"I must admit," Beverly declared, "that the roving life fascinates me."

"You have the gypsy heart," he said again. "You too love to travel to new places, you——"

"I would choose a more comfortable means of travel than a wagon," Beverly laughed. "I'm all bumps and bruises from my few days as your—guest."

"You are bitter against the gypsies," he sighed. "We are a friendly people. Why do you hate us?"

"Should I love my kidnapers?" the girl demanded. "You can't expect a prisoner to love his jailer. Of course I hate the gypsies, and when I get back to my friends I shall send the police after Dimiti at once."

The young man shook his head. "Dimiti knows that, and he will not let you go."

"Sooner or later," Beverly said confidently, "he will relax his vigilance and I will escape."

"You could escape now," he said slowly. "You could run away from me, and perhaps I could not find you again."

"If I did, it would cause trouble between you and Dimiti, wouldn't it?" Beverly demanded.

He nodded. "Dimiti would most certainly run his knife into me."

"You are my only friend in the gypsy camp," Beverly said shaking her head, "and I never let my friends down."

He smiled. "You have a keen sense of honor. Look!"

A red autogiro was swooping low over the trees where they were walking. There were two men in the plane, their heads and shoulders could just be seen above the edges of the cockpits.

"What a strange plane!" the gypsy remarked.

Beverly laughed at his mystification. "It is an autogiro. Have you ever been up in an airplane?"

Anselo shook his head. "No. I would be afraid to

trust myself to such a fragile thing thousands of feet above the earth. Have you ever been up?"

Beverly nodded. "It is thrilling. It makes one feel almost like a bird."

The gypsy smiled. "I am content with being a man. I like the feel of the solid earth beneath my feet."

The plane was circling around overhead, and the two stood still to watch it. It was swooping lower, lower until the wheels barely missed the tops of the tall trees.

"He is going to land in the road beyond our camp," Anselo said. "Perhaps there is something wrong."

The plane was out of sight now. Beverly was thinking of the lettering on the side of the cockpit. It had been easily discernible when the plane swooped low, and it struck a familiar note in her memory. The *Red Bird II*. Where had she heard of a plane by that name before? Of course! Larry Owens, the Secret Service agent, had gotten a new plane and christened it *Red Bird II*. Was he looking for her? He was landing near the gypsy camp. Did that signify anything? Was he tracing the gypsies to find her? It seemed the most logical explanation.

"Let us go and see the plane on the ground," she

said, turning to Anselo, suppressed eagerness in her voice.

He shook his head. "No. We are too far from the road now."

"Let us turn back," she pleaded.

"No," he said again.

It was then the plane soared into the sky again. Did she imagine it, or did Anselo actually look relieved? The plane went for a short distance to the north, banked sharply, and turned back again. Once more the plane landed on the road. Beverly turned and began making her way back the way they had come.

Anselo caught her arm. "Where are you going?"

"I'm going back to the wagon," she answered.

"No," he said shortly, "you must not go back there."

A thought occurred to her, and she faced him angrily. "They are men looking for me, aren't they?"

He nodded. "Dimiti had word that the police would search our camp today."

"That is why he had you bring me out here in the woods," she exclaimed suddenly. "You brought me here so that the men wouldn't find me when they looked through the wagons."

He nodded.

Beverly faced him contemptuously. "And I thought you were my friend!"

Anselo's face was set. "You do not understand. Dimiti and the other men planned to involve your friends in a quarrel and perhaps kill them, if they found you in the camp. I suggested taking you out of sight to avert bloodshed."

The young man spoke slowly, sincerely, and Beverly felt her anger melting away. Dimiti had planned to kill Larry—and whoever the man was that was with him, so Anselo had tricked her into taking a walk with him. Rescue was so near and yet so many miles away. Even as she stood there, the roar of the plane was heard, and the autogiro rose in the sky. The plane circled once over the camp and then streaked away into the north. There went all her hopes of a rescue from the gypsies. They had searched the gypsy camp once, there would be no need of any further search. Larry and the others would not now expect her to be with the gypsies. They had found nothing in the camp, so their suspicions would be calmed.

That meant that she might have to stay in the camp, a prisoner, for days, even weeks, to come. She had no hope now of rescue by her friends, so she would have to plan every minute for an escape. But how? How could she escape when they kept the wagon door always barred?

Anselo, as they walked slowly back to the camp, looked down at the girl by his side. "You are very quiet," he said slowly. "Are you angry with me?"

"No," Beverly answered. "You were acting under Dimiti's orders when you tricked me into leaving the camp."

"Believe me, it was no trick. Of course, I know you consider it so," he acknowledged, "because by now your friends have left. But I really wanted to walk with you."

Beverly smiled but said nothing. He was her friend, but all the same he was a gypsy, and his loyalty to his tribe came first. They completed the walk to the camp in silence. Beverly was conscious of the broad, relieved smiles of the other gypsies when she entered her wagon and the door was barred behind her. They were extremely pleased with themselves. The police had searched their camp and found nothing; they were safe.

She sat down on her bunk and buried her face in her hands. Slow tears trickled down her cheeks. It was the first time during all her captivity that she had allowed herself the consolation of tears. Beverly was not usually the crying kind, but now she felt particularly hopeless and beaten. She had scarcely realized just how much she had counted on her friends' finding her. Now she felt lost and utterly crushed. She had no hopes to cling to, and nothing to console her. She was utterly at the mercy of the gypsies, and with Dimiti as the leader, what might they not do with her? He was a ruthless man, and even Anselo, as her friend, could not defy Dimiti for her sake.

Someone was coming in, and Beverly turned hastily to the window. She would not let the gypsies guess she had been crying. Never would she show them a beaten front! She would be defiant and confident in their presence. The woman brought her supper and withdrew. Beverly scarcely touched the food. Somehow it seemed to choke her tonight. She could think of nothing but the helpless position in which she found herself. The woman returned and removed the dishes. Beverly continued to stare out the window. She leaned her head wearily against the casement and let the evening breezes cool her hot cheeks. She stood there until the last dying rays of the setting sun had faded and the stars came out one by one. The moon rose, throwing the trees into black relief against the sky.

What were her friends thinking back at Vernon? What were her parents doing? How she longed for the comforting arms of her mother at that moment! Had they given up hope of ever finding her, as she had almost given up hope of ever returning to them? What were the Alphas doing?

The Alphas! The six of them had had a lot of good times together. Would she ever see them again, she wondered? The Alpha Delta Sorority had become one of the most popular groups on the Vernon campus. The other girls envied the staunch friendship that held the group together. Would they get another girl to take her place? Somehow she didn't think they would, at least not right away. The friendship she had had for the girls and they for her would not easily die. They were a curious group, their natures so widely different. Surely the saying was right—"Opposites attract." She could not say what it was had drawn them together. Day after day they had continued to meet and play and study together until it seemed the most natural thing in the world for the six of them always to go places together. The six Alphas had become a moving light in the world of sports and studies. They were popular figures in every phase of college life. But now there were only five. She was not there, and she wondered what they were doing. Were they continuing with their fun? She hoped so. Even though she were not there, she didn't want to deprive her friends of anything.

The sweet, rhythmic strains of a mellow violin broke in upon her unhappy thoughts. Anselo and his fiddle! He came closer to her window, as he had done the night before. But tonight the music did not charm her. She listened and liked it, but it could not carry her away into dreams. Tonight the spell seemed broken. He played long, and she listened silently. The moon rose high in the sky, and the gypsy camp fire died down. Finally he brought his concert to a close and went away. Beverly retired to her bunk and lay there, thinking. It was long before she could smother her unhappy thoughts and fall asleep.

The gypsies were on the move early in the morning. The sun was particularly bright today, but even so the world looked dark to Beverly. She still felt dejected about what had happened yesterday. Somehow she could summon no happy thoughts to rescue her from her depression. At noon the gypsies stopped. In the distance could be heard the hum of many voices, and the whirr of activity was in the air. Beverly wondered if they were near a town. If they were, perhaps she could find some way to escape! That was the first thought that occurred to her, but it was superseded by another. Most likely the gypsies would keep her locked in the wagon all day. They would take no chances of having her get away from them now.

The woman brought her luncheon, and then the camp grew quiet. It almost seemed deserted. Had the gypsies all left, or were they merely taking an afternoon siesta? Beverly paced nervously back and forth. If there was only some way in which she could leave this hateful wagon. She had tried the door and found it securely bolted.

"Hello!" Anselo's voice came to her, and she looked up to see him smiling in the window.

"Hello!" she responded, not ungraciously. "Everything seems so quiet, I thought the gypsies had gone away and left my wagon deserted here," she continued lightly.

"There is a fair over beyond the trees," he explained. "Orlenda is telling fortunes, and Dimiti is trading horses."

Beverly said nothing, and after a while he continued.

"Would you care to go over to the Fair?" he asked hesitantly. "Of course, Dimiti must not see us, or he will be very angry. There is much fun and laughter there."

"Of course I would like to go," Beverly said promptly. "And I don't care whether Dimiti sees me or not."

"But," Anselo hesitated, "you must promise me that you will not try to run away."

It was a long minute before Beverly answered. It had seemed a chance to escape. In the crowd of people she could easily slip away from Anselo, but if she promised him not to—well, she always kept her promises.

"Very well, I promise," she said finally.

"And I know you will not break that promise," he said smiling.

It was something to get out of her wagon prison even for a few hours. They did not follow the road to the Fair, but cut across the fields and came up beside the tents of the side shows. There was the tent with the fat lady, the sword swallower, the fire eater, the snake charmer—it was almost like a circus. Popcorn stands were in profusion. She and Anselo enjoyed a hot dog and a bottle of soda pop while they watched the snake charmer and her slimy pets. Flags waved gayly overhead, and in the distance was the sound of a band playing. Crowds jammed the midways, and they were scarcely able to breathe for the dust and heat. They passed close to where Orlenda had set up her fortune-telling tent, but they did not see any of the gypsies, and for that they were both thankful.

They paused to watch the sword swallower as he demonstrated his marvelous feat. For a moment Beverly's gaze wavered from the scene before her and traveled across the road to where another girl was standing, staring at her. Her heart leapt in her throat. Was it? It was! Gerry Foster! Gerry had graduated from Vernon College only last June, and she had been a close friend of Beverly and all the Alphas. The girl was staring at her so strangely that Beverly doubted if Gerry recognized her. Anselo spoke to her then, and she faintly heard his voice.

"Dimiti has seen us. We must hurry away."

She nodded and with a final look at Gerry and a half smile she turned to follow Anselo. She had met an old friend and had not been recognized. A wry smile twisted her lips as she hurried with Anselo back to her wagon. She had had hopes that Gerry would recognize her and notify her friends, but things were against her. She seemed doomed to live forever as a member of the gypsy tribe. She had been honor bound by her promise to Anselo not to try to escape, and she had kept that promise. All she could do now was to hope that Gerry *had* recognized her and would send word to Vernon that she, Beverly, was in this vicinity. Surely she had recognized the fact that Anselo was a gypsy! That would give the authorities and her friends a clue. If she had been with a gypsy, there was but one conclusion to draw.

They reached her wagon, and she entered, and Anselo bolted the door after her. So far they had

not met any of the other gypsies. But Anselo had
said Dimiti saw them. That meant that there was
trouble in the air. Anselo would no doubt be up-
braided for having taken her out of the gypsy
camp. He had done it as a kindness toward her, and
she would not let him get in trouble if she could
help it.

It was late in the afternoon when the door to her
wagon was thrown open and Dimiti stalked in. He
was in a towering rage, as one look at his face
showed her. The storm was about to break. She
stood quietly at ease while he glared at her.

"Anselo will take you to no more fairs," he shot
at her viciously.

The thought that he might have killed her one
friend here shook her. "What have you done to
him?" she asked, trembling.

Dimiti laughed, a cruel, remorseless laugh that
chilled her blood. "I have slashed him with my
knife, so—and so——" The blade of his knife
swished through the air as he demonstrated how
he had applied it to Anselo.

The thought sickened her, and she turned her
head away.

"Ah, you do not like that," he said, advancing a
step while she drew farther away. He laid his knife
down on the table and continued to advance on

her. "The next time you want to go to a fair, my little one, you ask Dimiti, eh? Dimiti will take you. We could be very good friends."

He put out his hand to stroke her arm, but she pulled away. The loathing that she felt for him showed itself in her eyes, and he frowned.

"Keep away from me," she said through clenched teeth. As he continued to advance, she backed away until she was against the table. Quite by accident her fingers came in contact with his knife. She grasped it firmly. The man made a sudden lurch at her, and she thrust the knife at him. It went deep into the flesh of his upper arm.

Blind rage and pain took possession of him. He staggered back, and she dropped the knife—horror stricken. He struck her a vicious blow and caught her unawares. She staggered backward from the impact and stumbled over one of the boxes that was used for a chair. She crashed to the floor and, in falling, struck her head on the side of the bunk and lay still, perfectly still. The gypsy stood over her, a scowl on his face and the knife gripped in his hand.

CHAPTER XII

Prisoners

THE AUTOGIRO rose into the evening sky like a bird ready for flight. Larry flashed a grin over his shoulder at Jim and set his course. It was less than an hour since they had learned of Gerry's glimpse of Beverly at the County Fair, and they were on their way. They had lost no time in climbing into flying togs and fueling the airplane. At last the star of hope was burning brightly for them, and they chafed at any delay.

The Alpha girls had all trooped down to the airport to watch them take off. The young men leaned over the side and waved. The motor hummed rhythmically, and the propeller cut through the air like a knife. Speed and more speed was what Larry wanted, and he drove his little plane forward as fast as he could. It would take at least an hour and a half before they reached the town where the Fair had been, and it might take some time after that before they could locate the gypsy camp. But they would do it. This time they would not declare themselves openly to the gypsies as they had done the last time. They would sneak up on the tribe under cover of the night and take them by surprise. This time they would have no time to hide Beverly, as they must have done the last time. Both young men had mental pictures of what they would like to do to the gypsies.

Inspector Dugan had sent word to the authorities in that little town in Pennsylvania to be on the lookout for the gypsies, but the young men hoped that they would reach the camp before the police did. They wanted to be the ones to rescue Beverly from the gypsies' clutches.

Miles and town after town passed beneath them. The sun had set when at last they flew over what was the remains of the Fair. The side shows were gone, and one by one the stands were being taken away. The flags had disappeared, and the only people present were the workmen.

Larry landed his plane in a cow pasture not far from the Fair grounds, and together the two made inquiries about the gypsies.

"Wal, now," the man of whom they had asked their questions said slowly, "it seems to me I saw the gypsies and their wagons leavin' right early this mornin'."

"Which way did they go?" Jim demanded quickly.

"They took the main road," the man answered.

"But did they go north or south, east or west?" Larry asked impatiently. "We don't care which road they took. We are going to follow them in a plane."

"An airplane?" the man asked aghast. "Gosh, what did they do, mister?"

"I'll write you a letter about it," Larry promised, his patience hanging by a thread, "but which way did they go?"

"To the north," the man answered. "They have a regular camping place in the hills. They go there every year."

"That's where we're going," Larry said promptly. "Thanks for the information. Come on, Jim."

The two young men ran back to the plane, and it roared into the sky, while the workman stared in open-mouthed awe after it. Larry kept his plane directly over the road, and Jim trained field glasses on the ground to pick up sight of the gypsy camp. It was growing darker, and it was ever increasingly difficult to determine objects on the ground. Occasionally patches of yellow light signified a house below them. The moon rose, and its silver spread over the world, throwing the trees and bushes into dark relief.

They were passing over a thickly wooded area, and the road wound up and down over hills and valleys. The workman had said the gypsy camp was in the hills. Three times Larry sent his autogiro speeding over the hills while the two strained their eyes to pick up some trace of a camp. A strong wind had sprung up, and the air was chill. Suddenly a spurt of color in the darkness below told them a fire was burning brightly. It must be in a cave, or it would be visible all the time and not only when a gust of wind sent it mounting higher.

Larry signaled that he was going to land. He had to fly over the hills and land his plane in a meadow. The two hopped out almost before the propeller had stopped turning.

"Make no noise and don't show a light," Larry instructed. "We are going to surprise that gang this time."

"Right you are," Jim said firmly. "I'm aching to get my hands on that fellow we met the other day."

"You and me both," Larry said grimly, starting off in the direction of the hills.

They went slowly, for the meadow was full of treacherous holes in the ground. From the air the meadow did not seem a great distance from the foothills, but it took them precious, impatient minutes to cover it. They crept forward silently and once Jim stumbled loudly over a rock. They stopped in their tracks and waited for a gypsy to spring up before them, but none did. They went on then, creeping forward stealthily. The ground sloped upward, and they knew they would soon come to the rocky mountain side.

Now it was necessary to move with extreme caution if they hoped to take the gypsies by surprise. A misstep would send a loose pebble slipping down over the rocks and awake a million echoes. They climbed over the boulders as silently as possible. They had discovered a place where they could creep between overhanging rocks and so save themselves the time and labor it took to climb up the hill and down the other side. They paused at the opening and crouched low, looking down on the gypsies camped almost at their feet.

The wagons were drawn into the customary circle, but the camp fire was, as they had suspected, built in a cave on the hillside and not in the center of the ring of wagons, as usual. The gypsies lounged on the wagon steps, and a few sat about the fire in the cave.

"Where do you suppose Beverly is?" Jim whispered.

Larry pointed down below. "See? That same wagon is drawn a little apart from the others. My guess is that Beverly is in there."

"We'll rush it," Jim proposed.

"If we get a chance," Larry reminded him. "I think the gypsies will keep a close watch on her."

"What do you think we should do?" Jim frowned. "It is hardly possible to sneak up to the wagon. Someone is sure to see us."

"We'll take that chance," Larry said. "Come on, we'll keep close to these trees until we get around to the wagon."

"Righto, I'm with you," Jim responded cheerily.

They left the foothills and crept along in the shadows of the trees. Everything was fine until a particularly hard gust of wind sent the fire leaping upward, and the light plainly revealed the two young men skulking along in the shadows. Three gypsies sprang up simultaneously and bore down on Jim and Larry. The latter two stood their ground firmly. They did not propose to run. They had come to find Beverly, and they were not going to leave without her!

"So, you are spying on the gypsies, eh?" It was the man Beverly knew as Dimiti who spoke. He carried his right arm in a sling, and a bandage bulged out his jacket sleeve.

Jim and Larry remained silent. They were watching the other gypsies as they closed in on them.

"What do you want here?" Dimiti continued.

"You have a girl prisoner here," Larry said in a low voice.

"We've come for her," Jim continued.

The gypsies exchanged glances. Dimiti smiled. "There is no girl here. You were present the other day when the police searched our camp, were you not? You saw that they found nothing."

"Just the same, we think she is here," Larry said grimly.

"Do you see her?" Dimiti asked insolently.

"No," Jim admitted, "but we are not leaving until we have searched the camp."

"You have no cause to search the camp," Dimiti said, his voice heavy with anger.

"Nevertheless, we are going to," Larry said firmly. "And we will start with that wagon over there." He motioned to the wagon that was drawn a little apart from the others.

"No." Dimiti took a menacing step forward and his men closed in behind him. "You will not search the camp. You will leave—now!"

Larry almost smiled. "We aren't leaving," he said confidently. "Not unless you produce that girl immediately."

Larry and Jim exchanged glances and moved away. One of the gypsies stepped in front of Larry and pushed him back. Larry chose to take offense at the push, and he launched a punch at the gypsy's jaw. That started a grand scrimmage. The gypsies piled on Jim and Larry, one after the other. The young men fought like tigers, and more than one gypsy disclosed a black eye or a broken tooth where he had come in contact with a flying fist. Larry and Jim were really overcoming the tremendous odds against them when a gypsy who carried a large club entered the quarrel. Two blows from the club, and the two young men were lying senseless, side by side, on the ground.

Dimiti walked over and kicked Larry disgustedly. "Throw them in the cave, the dogs," he ordered his men. "Bind them. We will give them a chance to think over their sins."

Larry's and Jim's hands and feet were bound

securely, and they were thrown into a dirty, evil-smelling cave.

"Ooooo, my head!" Jim rolled over and struggled to sit up.

"Mine feels the same way," Larry murmured. "We walked into a nice mess, didn't we?"

"A big help we are to Beverly," Jim groaned. "Of all the fools——"

"We take the cake," Larry finished for him. "Gosh, this place is damp!"

The ground was moldy, and they were chilled to the bone. It was so dark that they could not even determine where the opening was by which to enter the cave.

"They should furnish a light," Larry grumbled. "Then we could tell what kind of a dump we are in."

"How long do you think they will keep us here?" Jim asked.

"I wish I knew," answered Larry. "At least we have some consolation in knowing that the police, too, are on the way here."

"If the gypsies stay here," Jim reminded him. "We have warned them now. It would be easy for them to skip out."

"Oh, what can we do?" Larry grumbled. "We were the dumbbells! If that fellow with the club hadn't joined the outfit, we would have cleaned them up."

"It is a good thing for us he used a club instead of a knife," Jim declared. "Things might be a lot worse."

"I don't think so," answered Larry gloomily. "We are in a fine pickle now. If Beverly is here, we haven't one chance in a thousand of getting to her."

"What was that?" Jim whispered after a moment of silence.

"What was what?" Larry demanded. "I didn't hear anything."

"I did. There it is again, someone is coming."

"And not making any noise about it," Larry added. "Hope he isn't coming to finish us off."

"Cheerful!" Jim rebuked. "Keep quiet a minute and listen."

A soft pad, pad of feet came to them as a man ran toward the cave in which they lay. A dark figure crept within.

"Gentlemen," the newcomer whispered.

"That's us," spoke up Larry. "And if you have come here with one of those carving knives to finish us off——"

"No," the voice said, and there was a suspicion of a smile in it. "I have come as a friend."

"Surprise," murmured Larry.

"Are you bound?" the voice asked, and the man came farther into the cave.

"Do you think we are sitting here because we like the scenery?" Jim demanded irritably.

The man crept forward, and a knife slashed through the thongs that bound Jim's hands and feet. In a moment Larry too was free.

"I say, who are you?" Larry asked. "This is sporting of you."

"Do not speak too loudly," the man cautioned. "The gypsies have sharp ears."

"But who are you?" Jim insisted. "We would like to know."

"It does not matter," the other answered. "You came to help Beverly Gray?"

"You bet!" Larry and Jim exclaimed in unison.

"Then," the stranger led the way to the entrance of the cave and crouched there, "you see that wagon to one side of the camp?"

"Yes," again said the two young men.

"You will find her in there. There is a bar across the door, lift it quietly, and make no noise if you value your life—and hers."

Larry grasped the man's hand in his. "I don't know who you are, but all the same, we thank you."

"It is nothing. You see, I, too, am a friend of hers. You will go quickly, but be gentle with her, she has just now recovered from——"

Jim gripped his arm tensely. "Has any of these gypsies hurt her?"

"It is nothing," the man said again. "Go—go now, and quickly."

"But you—" Larry hesitated—"if the gypsies know you set us free they will kill you."

"No," the other said slowly, "they will not know I set you free. Go, and tell the girl—Anselo wishes her happiness always."

Reluctantly the two young men turned from the cave. They were loath to leave their rescuer, but he wished it so. Besides, in a moment they would be with Beverly. Their endless days of search would be over.

CHAPTER XIII

Escape

BEVERLY sat up and passed a hand dazedly across her eyes. Her head ached alarmingly, and she felt curiously light-headed. What had happened? Why was she lying on the floor instead of on her bunk? She stood up and swayed unsteadily. Why was the room spinning around so crazily?

It was then that the memory of the scene with Dimiti recurred to her. She remembered thrusting the knife into him, and she remembered his striking her, but after that everything was blurred. She must have given her head an awful crack. Her exploring fingers drew an exclamation of pain from her as they came in contact with a bump on the back of her head.

The door was locked, and darkness had descended on the world outside. It must be hours since she and Anselo had returned from the Fair. Evidently she was to get no supper tonight, for there were no signs of anyone stirring in the gypsy camp. Her thoughts came back to Anselo. Dimiti had said he slashed him with his knife. How horrible! The man was utterly heartless. Anyway, she felt a slight satisfaction in knowing that she had run his own knife into him. She hoped sincerely that Anselo wasn't much hurt. The young man had been good to her, and she really liked him.

Beverly lay down on the bunk and rested her aching head on the flat pillow. What would happen now? Dimiti would hate her more than ever now that she had knifed him. What would he do? She shivered when she thought of the anger that had blazed at her from his eyes. He was capable of anything! Murder, to him, would mean less than nothing. He was a fine leader for a lawless tribe.

Her memory went leaping back to that afternoon when she had seen Gerry Foster. She built her hopes high on her friend. If only she would notify the authorities! Surely her friends would search the gypsy camp again. Her thoughts together with her aching head kept her awake long into the night.

The gypsy wagon had begun to move when she

awoke in the morning. It was the jolting that had roused her. She sat up and rubbed her head reflectively. It did not ache as much as it had last night, but there was still a bruise there that hurt when her fingers came in contact with it. The sun was high in the heavens, and she was hungry. She hoped the gypsies didn't intend to starve her. She had had nothing to eat since yesterday, when she and Anselo had enjoyed a hot dog. She went to the window and looked out. They were passing through the Fair grounds. The shows were gone, and men were dismantling the remaining stands. Where were they bound for now? she wondered. Every day they drew farther and farther away from Vernon. Would her friends ever catch up with her?

The wagon stopped late in the afternoon. From her window she could see that they were near foothills. Was this a permanent camp, or would they be on the move again tomorrow? The woman brought her supper, and Beverly was acutely aware of the dark glances she cast in the girl's direction. The woman would cheerfully have poisoned her, Beverly declared to herself. She probably felt so because she, Beverly, had stuck a knife into the leader of the band, Dimiti. After the woman took away the soiled dishes, Beverly took up her stand at the window. They had changed the position of her wagon tonight. She could now see a portion of the camp. She wondered if Anselo would play his violin for her tonight. She wondered if he were able to play, or had Dimiti hurt him severely?

As she stood there a familiar humming noise came to her. The sun had long since faded, and the moon was bright in the sky. An airplane was flying overhead. She had one joyous hope that it might be Larry again. But it was only yesterday that she had seen Gerry. Of course she had had time to write to someone at Vernon, but how had they traced the gypsies so quickly? The plane did not stop near the camp, though, but continued on. The humming faded into the distance, and silence settled down.

A man crept to her wagon through the darkness and lounged beneath her window. She could see that he had several white strips of bandage across part of his face.

"Anselo!" she murmured in quick sympathy. "Dimiti did hurt you!"

"It is nothing." The young man shrugged, but his voice was not as buoyant as usual. "Did he harm you?"

"No," Beverly answered.

"But I saw him strike you," Anselo contradicted. "I watched beneath this very window and saw you lying on the floor so white and still."

"He didn't hurt me as much as I hope I hurt him. Does his arm hurt?"

Anselo grinned in the darkness, and he almost laughed as he spoke. "Ah, you are indeed a spitfire. Dimiti's arm is wounded sorely, and his pride more so. He paces back and forth before the camp fire muttering to himself, and even Orlenda cannot calm him."

"Look, Anselo, who are they?"

"Who are who?" the gypsy asked.

"There in the shadows are two men, see them?" Beverly whispered excitedly.

Two vague, shadowy forms had just come into sight, slipping from tree to tree. They couldn't be two of the gypsy tribe, because they moved so stealthily. They seemed a part of the shadows themselves.

"I see them," Anselo answered, "but I do not know who they might be."

At the same moment that the two young people saw the strangers, the gypsies saw them. Anselo and Beverly watched breathlessly while the gypsies surrounded the strangers. The camp fire surged up brightly, and occasionally it flung a bright glare over the group of men.

"They are aviators," Beverly said joyously. "It must be Larry!"

"They are not friends," Anselo confirmed. "Dimiti is angry."

"Perhaps they are my friends," Beverly said in a hopeful voice.

Anselo slipped away from the wagon and crept through the trees until he could overhear what the intruders were saying. He listened to every word spoken by Larry and Jim and Dimiti. When Larry struck the gypsy and the fight began, Anselo retreated. He did not propose to join in any quarrel tonight. He had his own troubles, and besides, he wanted to help Beverly. He knew the men were her friends, but he could not help them in any way now. He went back and took up his stand beneath Beverly's window once more.

"Who are they?" Beverly demanded breathlessly.

"Watch," was all he said.

The two watched while the battle raged. The camp was a mass of struggling, squirming figures. It was difficult in the dim light to tell one man from the other. They saw the gypsy with the club wield his weapon and one man crumple from the blow, and then saw him swing on the other.

"That's not fair!" Beverly cried, gripping Anselo's shoulder tensely.

"What can we do?" he asked.

The gypsies carried the two men out of Beverly's

range of vision, but Anselo communicated the news to her.

"They are taking your friends to a cave on the hillside," he said.

"My friends!" Beverly echoed. "Were they my friends?"

Anselo nodded. "They came for you."

He described the two men, and Beverly listened with bated breath. One was Larry: the description fitted him perfectly. The other sounded, oh, so much like Jim! But Jim should be back in Renville. Larry and Jim—prisoners of the gypsies.

"Anselo! What can we do?" she cried. "We must help them!"

He shook his head slowly. "I can help them to escape, but if they came for you and Dimiti discovered them, he would kill the two."

Beverly hesitated, but only for an instant. Her choice was clear to her. Anselo was right. Dimiti would kill the two young men if they attempted to help her escape. Therefore there was only one thing left to do. They must save themselves. She wanted to get away from the gypsy camp, of course, but she couldn't let two of her best friends risk their lives for her. Eventually she might be able to escape by herself. Now her concern was for the safety of Jim and Larry. They must get away before Dimiti took it into his head to kill them. She knew he was cruel, and he would not stop at murder.

"Anselo," she said urgently, "you must help me."

"I am your friend," he said slowly.

"Then—help those two to escape. Tell them to leave the camp at once. Tell them that I am not here—tell them anything, but make them go before Dimiti kills them!"

"But you——"

"It does not matter about me. Dimiti will not harm me, and I am not afraid to stay here. Will you, Anselo? Please, help them to escape—for my sake."

"For your sake I would do anything," he said slowly.

"Then—show them how to leave the camp without Dimiti seeing them."

"I will wait until the gypsies have retired for the night," Anselo whispered, "then I will go and help them." He bent low over her hand with a touch of Old World gallantry. "Good-night."

"Good-night," Beverly responded, "and—thank you."

She watched Anselo's figure fade into the darkness, and then she turned and flung herself down upon the bunk. She had probably saved Jim and Larry, but at what a cost. Would she never be able to leave this despicable wagon? Rescue had been within reach, and she had sent it away. Anselo would keep his word and help Jim and Larry. Of that she had no doubts. But would they go without her? She hoped so, even though it meant days more of captivity for her. It was better that they should go without her than to have Dimiti kill them. Why did that thought persist in taunting her?

She lay there in the darkness listening to the merriment that emanated from the gypsies. For some reason they were in high spirits tonight. Music, laughter, and song filled the air for many hours. She began to fear that Anselo would never have a chance to make his way to the cave in which lay Larry and Jim. Finally the music and the laughter began to die away, and soon silence had settled over the camp. Was he now creeping toward the cave?

In her thoughts she followed every step and every movement that Anselo would be making. Now he would be stalking in the shadows. The next moment he was bending over Jim and Larry. Would they believe him when he told them she was not in the camp? She didn't think so. But whether they believed him or not, if only they would return to the plane and fly away! She could not rest in peace until she heard the plane overhead and knew that at last they were on their way. Why, oh, why didn't Anselo hurry? Surely it was safe for him now to go to the cave? Had he forgotten about it?

The minutes and the hours passed while she lay still, straining her ears for the sound of a plane motor. There was not a sound of anyone moving in the gypsy camp. Perhaps Larry and Jim had left the plane at a great distance. If that was the case, she would not be able to hear the motor when it started. That was all there was left to hope for. It would scarcely have taken this long for Anselo to reach and set them free.

A scratching noise at the door of her wagon brought her upright. She crouched tensely on the edge of the bunk, straining her eyes into the darkness. Was it Dimiti? The remembrance of his uncontrollable anger came to her, and she shivered. What did he mean, coming to her wagon now when everyone in the camp was asleep? Had he come to take revenge for her stabbing him? The door was opened slowly, and a dark form appeared on the threshold.

"Beverly—are you there?"

Beverly knew the familiar voice well, and she flung herself on the young man, burying her head on the broad shoulder.

"Jim—oh, Jim——" she whispered, the thankful tears stinging her eyes.

"Did you think we would go away without you?" he asked, stroking the curly head gently.

"Hello, Beverly." Larry came into the wagon and threw exultant arms about her, giving her a bear hug. "Boy, it is dark in here."

"But why did you come for me?" Beverly wailed. "If Dimiti catches you he will kill you!"

"In that case we better scram," said Larry promptly. "I have no desire to be cut into sausages."

"Nor I," Jim said smiling. "Let's get out of here."

The two young men each grasped Beverly by an arm, and together the three left the wagon where Beverly had been so long a prisoner. They crept from the gypsy camp and into the foothills. A misstep on Larry's part sent a rock rolling down into the camp and set thunderous echoes alive in the hills. In the twinkling of an eye, the place had become alive with men. They hurried from the wagons, calling to one another to ascertain what the danger was. One of the men spied the three fugitives on the hillside, and the whole band started in pursuit.

"Good-night!" Larry wailed. "Look what we have to race now."

They found the overhanging rocks and crept between them. In a moment they were scrambling down the other side of the hill. Men began creeping through the opening and pursuing them. A sudden whizz past Larry's ear brought him to an abrupt halt. He stooped over and retrieved something from the ground.

"Look," he held up his prize. The moonlight gleamed on the blade of a knife. "Throwing knives at us," he said grimly. "I'm going to keep this one for a souvenir, and if I ever get the chance, I am going to stick it into the one who crowned me with that club."

They continued running until they had left the foothills behind them. When they came to the open field, at the farther end of which stood the autogiro, it was necessary to proceed with caution because of the many holes in the ground. Beverly's foot slipped into one of the rabbit holes, and she pitched forward to her knees.

"All right?" Larry and Jim demanded in unison as they lifted her between them.

"I—I've twisted my ankle," Beverly murmured, "but that won't keep us back. Come on."

"Don't run on it," Jim said quickly. "We will carry you."

The two young men made a chair seat of their hands and with an arm across each of their shoulders, Beverly was carried to the plane. They had to run fast, for the gypsies were hot on their trail. Jim lifted Beverly to the rear cockpit and climbed in beside her. Larry jumped into the pilot's seat and in short time had the motor running. He drove the plane straight at the pursuing gypsies, and they scattered like sand before a wind.

The plane rose gently into the sky just as the first streaks of dawn were appearing over the eastern horizon. Jim smiled down at Beverly, and she leaned her head wearily on his shoulder. It felt so good to know she was safe at last with friends. It would not be long before she would be back at Vernon—and wouldn't the girls be surprised!

CHAPTER XIV

Return

"WELL, there they go," Lenora said inconsequentially.

"You're telling us," observed Lois, craning over her friend's shoulder to get a last final glimpse of the *Red Bird II* as it faded over the horizon.

"I hope they have good news when they come back," Shirley observed.

The girls had accompanied Jim and Larry to the airport when they took off on their pursuit of the gypsies. Little did they realize that the search would end so happily.

"If we don't hear something soon," Lenora declared as they turned back to College Avenue, "I'll go jump in a lake—or something."

"Won't that be a calamity?" Lois murmured heartlessly.

Lenora frowned on her, to no avail. "I want you

to understand, my dear young lady, that I, as president of the Alpha Delta Sorority, resent your defamatory remarks."

"Oh-ho," Lois was beginning laughingly when Rosalie and Anne interfered.

"See here," Anne said, "if you two are going to start one of your arguments, I won't walk with you."

"Anne is right," Rosalie declared. "You are always grumbling. Can't you be together peacefully for ten minutes?"

"Lois, they don't appreciate us," wailed Lenora.

"Imagine," Lois joined in tearfully, "they say we are always grumbling. I don't grumble at all, it is you who——"

"Me?" Lenora shouted. "I like that! If it wasn't for me, who would——"

"There you go," Shirley interrupted. "Off again!"

Lenora and Lois grinned cheerfully and twined arms. They beamed on the others.

"Now, aren't we the picture of perfect companionship?" Lenora demanded.

"How long will it last?" Anne asked, unconvinced.

"Until Lenora makes one of her terrible wisecracks," Lois answered.

"See here," Lenora declared, "my wisecracks aren't terrible. It is you who is always——"

"Come on, girls," Shirley said determinedly. "We will walk on the other side of the street."

Anne and Rosalie and Shirley crossed the street, and Lois and Lenora grinned in repentance.

"We'll be good," Lenora promised.

"Come over and see us sometime," Lois called.

"If you can behave, you may join us," conceded Rosalie.

Finally, after many more words tossed back and forth between them, the girls reunited at the college grounds and progressed up to Shirley's room together. There they distributed themselves at various angles and in comfortable positions on the bed and on cushions on the floor.

"How long do you suppose it will take them to find the gypsy camp?" Anne asked.

"That all depends where the gypsies are," answered Lois.

"Bright girl," murmured Lenora.

"What will they do if Beverly isn't in the gypsy camp?" Rosalie wanted to know.

"Probably come back here, and then we will be just where we started," Shirley answered.

"We won't think about that until we see them," said Lois promptly. "Remember what the man said about crossing the bridge before you came to it."

"What did he say?" asked Lenora.

"Um—er—I don't exactly remember," Lois said slowly.

"Are you sure it was a man who said it—whatever it was?" continued Lenora mischievously.

The dinner bell rang then and put an end to what threatened to be another discourse between Lois and Lenora. The five Alphas trooped down to the dinner table happier than they had been since Beverly disappeared. Their hopes were high, and they could be jolly while they had something to hope for. They spent the social hour after dinner chatting and singing with the other Chadwick Hall girls. When the study-hour bell rang they trooped away to delve into the mysterious and intricate depths of textbooks.

Shirley donned pajamas and threw herself across her bed with her literature book. She tried to concentrate on the printed page before her, but her mind wandered. Where were Jim and Larry now? Had they found Beverly? Were they even at this minute on the way back to Vernon? Larry had promised to telephone the minute they landed at the airport, even if it was midnight, and Mrs. Dennis had promised faithfully that she would call Shirley and the other Alpha members.

Shirley crossed to the window and looked out at the countless thousands of stars, like tiny windows in the heavens. The night was so calm and peaceful and yet so mysterious. The same moon and the same stars were shining down on Beverly —wherever she was. The secret of Beverly's whereabouts was known to those silver stars there above, and they kept their secret well. Shirley set her chin on clenched hands and her thoughts whirled about, miles away from the open book before her.

The lights-out bell rang, and Shirley obediently put out her lamp, but she did not go to bed. She remained by the window looking out at the still, cool October night. The trees and the buildings were black below her. Lights in the other dormitory houses flickered out, leaving the windows like sightless eyes staring out upon the world. There was a light in Miss Wilder's office yet. Possibly she was waiting for some word of Beverly. The Dean and Beverly's mother had been great friends, and Miss Wilder had a keen interest in Beverly. Beverly's disappearance had been a great trial to her. She felt badly about it because the girls were all under her care, and to have something like this happen to any one of the students was——

"Hello, snookums." Lenora poked her head in the door. "In bed yet?"

"Nope," Shirley said promptly. "Come in."

" 'Smatter? Can't you sleep?"

"No," Shirley sat down on the bed, "I'm too excited."

"You and me both," said Lenora promptly. "I feel as if I couldn't sleep all night."

"Nor I," Shirley yawned.

"Let's keep a midnight watch," Lenora proposed. "We'll take turns keeping awake so if news of Beverly comes we will be on hand."

"Fine," Shirley replied. "We'll lay here on the beds and talk."

The two lay back on the soft covers and for a few minutes kept up a lively chatter about school events. Gradually the conversation died down. The moon rose high above the clouds, and the hands on the little desk clock turned slowly.

"Are you still awake, Lenora?" Shirley whispered.

"Uh-huh," was the drowsy answer.

More minutes passed, and by now both girls had slipped into dreamland. They had forgotten their self-imposed watch, and tired nature was taking its toll. The moon slipped farther into the west. The stars faded one by one as a rosy dawn crept into the east. The pink glow crept into the little college room and played gently across the beds.

Shirley rolled over and sat up sleepily. She yawned prodigiously and cocked a drowsy eye at Lenora.

"Say," she poked her friend experimentally.

"Go 'way," Lenora implored.

Shirley aimed a pillow and caught her friend squarely in the face. Lenora sat up spluttering indignantly.

"What's the big idea?"

Shirley laughed. "Aren't we fine night watchmen?"

Lenora giggled. "Why didn't you stay awake?"

"For the same reason you didn't," Shirley said promptly. "The sandman caught me unawares."

"Ho-hum." Lenora stretched and stood up. "We might as well get up."

"I'm going down and see if Mrs. Dennis heard anything from Beverly," Shirley declared. "I don't see how we could have gone to sleep when we were so excited."

"Wait a moment, and I'll go along," Lenora said.

The two struggled sleepily through their showers and dressed, while they chattered on the possibilities of Beverly's return. They met Anne and Lois on their way to the dining room. The girls started coming down the stairs in groups, some with textbooks in their hands to sneak a last-minute glance at the lesson for the first period class.

Shirley went immediately to Mrs. Dennis' office but came back to the girls with no encouraging news. They all went into the dining room for their breakfast. The girls were in the middle of a heated discussion of the play to be produced in the spring half of the term, when the low hum of a motor filled the air.

"The *Red Bird!*" Lenora shouted excitedly and dived for the door.

Shirley was second to fly out to the campus, and the other girls followed with one accord. They stood on the campus, craning their necks for a glimpse of the red autogiro. They could hear the motor, but the plane was not in sight. Finally it appeared over Penfield Hall, and the girls cheered lustily, but for what reason they couldn't quite understand. They just had to make a noise or burst. The plane circled over the campus and glided down lower each time. The girls could see that there were three people in the cockpit, and they held their breath. Who was the third?

The campus was wide and the grass cut short. It made an excellent landing place for a plane, and Larry proceeded to set his autogiro down. The girls rushed toward it breathlessly. Larry jumped out first, and then Jim, and by the time the girls had arrived at the plane the third passenger was standing beside the two young men.

"Beverly!" Shirley cried and enveloped her chum with ecstatic arms.

Jim and Larry stood back and grinned as they watched the girls welcome their long lost classmate. They were disheveled and dirty from their fight with the gypsies and their subsequent sojourn in that damp, evil-smelling cave, but they were jubilant. Their brilliant smiles flashed through the dirt and grime.

"You've come back just in time for breakfast," Lenora said when the first breathless greetings were over.

"Lenora!" Anne exclaimed.

"Leave it to you to think of eats," Lois added.

"Well, I'll wager Beverly is hungry," Lenora defended.

"Of course I am," Beverly said promptly.

"And so are we," interposed Larry.

"Yes," Jim laughed, "don't the rescuers get any attention at all?"

"You certainly do," the girls exclaimed with one accord.

The three returned young people were marshaled into the dining room and installed in chairs at the head of the table. Everyone demanded that Beverly tell them the story of her kidnaping. Obligingly she supplied the details, and the girls listened with eagerness. Classes were forgotten for that morning, and Beverly held a reception for everyone. She was delighted and not a little awed at her popularity. All the girls and even the teachers told her how glad they were that she was back with them again.

Jim and Larry hovered in the background of all this jubilation. They enjoyed themselves immensely, even if the spotlight was not fastened upon them. They were pleased over being the instruments which had brought Beverly back to her friends. The jubilation kept up far into the night, and it was a day that was to go down in Vernon history. Beverly had been a heroine before, but now she was doubly one.

CHAPTER XV

Leaving

DURING the days that followed, Inspector Dugan did his best to find the gypsies. After Beverly's escape they had disappeared. Whether they had gone into hiding in the hills could not be determined. The authorities had combed the country surrounding the last camp site, but not a gypsy could be found. They had evaporated, as it were, into thin air and left not a trace behind them. Finally the search was given up as hopeless.

Beverly, in these days, was getting back into the stride of college routine after her forced absence. Once more she was eating and sleeping and studying as a care-free student, and not as a prisoner in a stuffy wagon. The story of her adventures was a never ending source of thrills and surprises for her friends, and time after time she had to recount the happenings for their benefit. They all declared they would have liked to meet Anselo, and Beverly herself often wondered what had become of him. Had Dimiti discovered that Anselo was responsible for Jim and Larry's escape—which led inevitably to her own? She might never know what became of him, but she would never forget his kindness to her. She would always remember the beauty and throbbing appeal of his violin playing; perhaps some day she would hear him play from a concert stage. He had the touch and musical ability that were bestowed only on the artist, and some day someone might discover him, and he would become a sensation in the musical world.

Something else had happened to her that made her feel thrilled and sorry at the same time. Larry, very haltingly and confusedly, had declared that he loved her and asked her to marry him. Beverly thrilled at the thought, as all girls do when they find someone loves them, but she was sorry, because she didn't love him in the same manner. She liked him—as a friend, but that was all.

It had happened two days after her return to the campus. He had asked her to take a walk in the woods with him. She had consented, and they had started off very light-hearted and gay. They had entered the woods that ran parallel behind the college buildings, laughing and chatting as two youngsters might who had been let out of school for a day. They had seated themselves momentarily on a fallen log, and there he had told her. Very gently and tenderly he had made the plea for what would mean lifelong happiness for him.

Beverly had been confused and surprised. Such a thought had never entered her mind for a moment. She had never suspected that there might be a hidden something behind Larry's care-free nonsense. She had hated to hurt him, but she really couldn't marry him. She told him, then, of her dreams for the future. She wanted to be a writer, and all her thoughts were for her career. She didn't want to marry anybody. She wanted to travel to all the far places in the world that she had read and dreamed about. She wanted to see the cherry blossoms in bloom in Japan, she wanted to see the Sphinx of Egypt, she wanted to see Monte Carlo, the Riviera—— Of course, a little house that would be all her own in the suburbs would be quite nice, but it wasn't for her. She wanted to roam across the world, dreaming and writing about the places that she visited. She wanted a career above everything else.

What was it Larry had said? Oh, yes, with a philosophical shrug he had turned to her and smiled.

"I'm sorry it couldn't be, Beverly," he had said. "You have wonderful dreams now, but some day— some day you will find that love can make up for all the things you think you want now."

And she had said, "Perhaps you are right, Larry." But she was unconvinced. She would stick to her determination to have a career. Just now she could think of nothing better than being a famous writer. The laurels of fame were infinitely alluring. No, she couldn't marry Larry. Perhaps it was heartless of her to be so determined against him, but she didn't want to marry anybody. She wanted Larry for a friend, but that was all.

She turned from the window in her room and made her way down to the campus. Jim was leaving this afternoon for Wyoming. All summer he had tried to obtain a position as engineer on a bridge-building project out there, and at last his opportunity had come. The bridge would take easily a year or more. The work he did on this, his first assignment, would determine the rest of his life. If he made good, he would be eligible for many other jobs where a young, successful engineer was needed.

She would miss Jim when he had gone. Yesterday Larry had left for New York, and now Jim was leaving. He would not be able to come home for the holidays as he had always done when he was in college. Before, when they had been separated for months, they met during vacation time. This was different. Jim was through with school now. He was no longer the boy she had played with, but a man with a man's job ahead of him. Of course, they would write to one another, but letters were always so unsatisfactory. One never seemed to be able to put on a piece of paper the thoughts one would confide to a person if one could see him.

Jim met her at the entrance to the college grounds, and they walked slowly toward the railway station. They chattered inconsequentially, mostly about little things. Somehow people never talk about the things they are really thinking when they are about to take leave of one another.

The train whistle sounded shrilly in the distance as they mounted the steps to the little wooden platform that did duty for a station.

"Well, Jim," Beverly said smiling, "you are on your way to your big opportunity. I wish you all the luck in the world! I know you will make good."

"Thanks, Beverly," Jim said, twisting his hat embarrassedly in his hands.

"What is the matter?" Beverly continued laughingly. "You have something on your mind. What is it? Can I help in any way?"

"Yes," Jim admitted, "you can help—a lot." But still he did not meet her glance squarely.

"What is it?" Beverly asked again. "The train is coming nearer. You have only a minute. Did you leave something in the hotel that you want me to send on to you? Have you forgotten anything?"

"No," Jim said reluctantly. "It is—just, well—we've been friends for a good many years."

"Ever since we started school," Beverly smiled.

"And—we've confided things in one another——"

"What? Is this a last minute confession?" Beverly demanded gayly. "I would never have suspected you, Jim, of any dark secrets in your past."

"Don't laugh," he rebuked seriously.

"I'm sorry, Jim," Beverly said quickly. "I didn't mean to. But what is it? Hurry, or you will miss your train."

Jim looked down the track where the limited was approaching ever nearer and turned back to her.

"When—during the time you disappeared, I became great friends with Larry—and the other day he told me he was going to ask you—to marry him."

"Yes," Beverly admitted slowly, "he did." Not to anyone but Jim would she have confessed it.

"Are you going to?" he demanded, and there was a tense eagerness about him that puzzled her.

"No," she said innocently. "I'm not going to marry him. I'm not going to marry anybody," she added.

Jim smiled broadly in relief. All his embarrassment had disappeared now that he had found out what he wanted to know, and he was his old cheery self.

"Everything is all right, then," he declared. "Everything is fine!"

"What do you mean—everything is fine?" Beverly asked. "Why were you so worried? Don't you like Larry?"

"Sure," Jim said magnanimously. "Sure, he is a great fellow. I'll tell you sometime what I was thinking about," he promised above the roar of the train as it pulled into the station.

When good-byes had been said and Jim's train was a mere blur in the distance, Beverly turned back to the college. What had been Jim's motive for asking that? Why had he waited so breathlessly for her answer? It was strange, today Jim had seemed different somehow.

She swung along College Avenue and met

Lenora and Lois. All her thoughts were dispelled from that moment on. The three went to Weller's, and Beverly had no more time to dwell on Jim's leaving. They met Shirley and Anne and Rosalie there, and the six proceeded to enjoy a rousing good time. After their sojourn at Weller's they all strolled back to Chadwick Hall and talked and sang with the other girls before dinner was served.

CHAPTER XVI

Holidays

BEVERLY entered her room from her conference with her literature teacher to find Shirley staring out the window, a crumpled letter in her hand.

"What's up?" she asked gayly. "You look very deep in thought."

"I was," Shirley laughed. "I've just received a letter from home. My parents are off to Europe."

"So what?" Beverly asked. "Did you want to go along?"

"No," Shirley answered, "but it leaves me rather at loose ends for Christmas. I wonder what I shall do?"

"Oh," Beverly said innocently, "didn't you know? You are coming home to Renville with me."

Shirley shook her head. "I couldn't impose on you."

"Impose? Impose?" Beverly echoed. "My dear girl, if it were in the least an imposition, I wouldn't ask you. I've wanted you to come for a long while, but I've been half afraid to ask you."

"Gracious, why?" Shirley said in surprise. "Am I that grizzly?"

"Of course not," Beverly laughed. "But Renville is a small town—it is almost country, in fact. You won't find it a bit like New York. You are used to the noise and confusion of the big city. Renville would seem strange to you."

"Not in the least," Shirley denied. "I spent one summer on a ranch in Arizona. Nothing could be more quiet than that. At night, any slight noise that we wouldn't even notice here sounds like an explosion out there."

"Then you will come home with me?" Beverly urged.

"I don't want you to think, because I said what I did, that I was angling for an invitation," Shirley said confusedly. "I was just thinking out loud."

"So much the better," Beverly answered. "But you will come, won't you? I want you to meet my mother and dad."

"I met your mother our first term here," Shirley reminded her, "and I'll be tickled to death to come."

"Fine!" Beverly beamed. "We'll have a high old time. Do you ice skate? Can you ski? Do you like coasting?"

"One at a time," Shirley laughed. "You forget, I was raised in the big city, and I'm not expert at outdoor sports as you are."

"We'll teach you," Beverly promised. "I'll write Mother today that you are coming home with me."

"Will she mind?"

"Of course not," Beverly smiled. "Mother doesn't mind a bit when I bring my friends home. That is one grand thing about her. I can pop up with anybody for dinner or lunch or the week-end and she won't be in the least bit disturbed. I don't think it would disturb her if I brought the King of Siam himself home with me."

Shirley laughed. "There is a thought. Why not ask him for Christmas?"

"I think we will be all filled up," Beverly added, giggling. "Perhaps he can come for the New Year."

The two girls settled down then to get in a few minutes' studying before dinner, and Beverly wrote her mother that she was bringing Shirley home for the holidays.

Accordingly Shirley, Beverly, and Anne, who too made her home in Renville, entrained for that dignified little suburban town a week later. They left the little station at Vernon amid cheers and the fluttering of handkerchiefs from the other Alpha members whose train did not leave until hours later. They had magazines and newspapers with which to content themselves until the train pulled into Renville. They had luncheon in the dining car and then buried themselves in their magazines again.

It was late in the afternoon, and the December sun was sinking swiftly when the three disembarked at the station. Beverly descended upon her parents like a young hurricane let loose. She threw rapturous arms about her mother and then her dad, at the same time breathlessly introducing Shirley to her dad and inquiring about all the home folks. Everything was laughs and kisses and confusion until they became conscious of the cold and hurriedly bundled into the Gray automobile to be whirled up the street to the house, all warm and cheerful.

Anne, meanwhile, had been set upon and whirled away by her own parents.

There was a huge fire roaring in the fireplace in the living room, and the Grays and their guest went toward it gratefully.

"Oh, the train was cold." Beverly shivered.

"The railroad companies never do heat their cars sufficiently," Shirley complained.

The two divested themselves of hats and coats and settled down on the divan before the fire, while Beverly's parents seated themselves in comfortable chairs on either side and demanded news of the college term. The girls obligingly supplied every bit of news, from additional anecdotes of Beverly's kidnaping by the gypsies to Lenora's latest wisecrack.

Dinner was served in the little dining room, and Beverly and Shirley insisted on helping to clear away the dishes. They made a game of it, and kept Mr. and Mrs. Gray amused and gay as they themselves were. After dinner they went again into the living room and turned on the radio and danced.

Mr. and Mrs. Gray might not be as young as their daughter in years, but their hearts were as lively as hers. They could enter into the fun of any of the young people, and the youngsters were quick to adore Beverly's parents. They idolized their daughter, but they had not spoiled her. They were understanding and sympathetic when she came to them with her problems, but they let her work them out her own way. They knew they could not hope to solve all her difficulties in the years to come, and it was best to get her used to self-reliance early in life. They gave her wise counsel and judgment when she asked for them, but never did they press their opinions on her.

The girls retired early, for they were tired from their journey. Beverly's room was not as sumptuous as the one she had shared last year in Shirley's New York home, but coziness and simplicity made up for what the room might lack in luxury. It seemed to reflect the girl's own cheerful, sunny personality, and Shirley declared herself charmed with it.

The following morning the girls unpacked their bags—they had been too tired to do it the night before—and after lunch the Lucky Circle descended on Beverly's home.

The Lucky Circle was a group of Beverly's friends, made up of Boyd Marshall, Tommy Chandler, Gordon Brewster, Jim Stanton, Joan Roberts, Barbara West, and Anne and Beverly. Jim was still in Wyoming working feverishly to make good at this, his first job. The Lucky Circle had incorporated under that name when they were all freshmen in high school, and during the years they had remained the best of friends.

They welcomed Shirley into their midst with the same breezy friendship they might have bestowed on a lifelong friend. The merriment echoed through the house until late, when they had to depart to their homes for dinner.

After dinner Shirley, Beverly, and her parents set up the Christmas tree in the corner of the living room. Mr. Gray climbed the stepladder to decorate the top of the tree, and the girls handed him generous amounts of tinsel and balls and lights. When, after several hours, it was finished, they stood back and surveyed their handiwork with satisfaction.

"Quite a work of art," declared Shirley modestly.

"The best we've ever had," Beverly added.

"But it gives you an appetite," said Mr. Gray.

"That means lunch," suggested Mrs. Gray.

"Lead us to it," begged Beverly.

After the midnight snack the girls retired to their room to sit in pajamas and discuss innumerable things. After a while they wandered to the window and stood looking out at the still world at their feet.

There was borne to them the clear, crystal sweetness of the church bells and the soft mellow tones of a Christmas carol. Overhead the Star of Bethlehem shone down with kindly brilliance. Gay wreaths hung in cottage windows, and candles were aglow. Every lighted window radiated good cheer and a friendly greeting to those passing by.

It was Christmas Eve all over the world. Everyone in the universe was echoing the yuletide spirit of good-will on earth to all men. The distant hills were hushed in the moonlight, and the little town lay silent in sleep.

The thought of Jim, away out in Wyoming, came to Beverly. It was the first Christmas she would not see him. Was he lonesome? Was he wishing himself back here with his friends? Was he looking up at the stars as she was, and feeling the infinite peace that descended on the world on this night? She had had a thick letter from him yesterday, and one from Larry.

"I'm glad I haven't any enemies," Shirley commented suddenly as they listened to a group of carol singers singing sweetly "Silent Night." "On Christmas I don't want anything but friends. Quarrels and hatreds seem so far away on Christmas Eve, I don't think I could quarrel tonight if I wanted to."

The singing died slowly in the distance as the singers moved on. The two girls stood together with arms twined about each other's waists. They were silent, just drinking in the beauty of the night. Somehow Christmas Eve always seemed the time to forget all the worries and cares and to dream about anything one liked. Why remember petty jealousies and strife when Christmas was meant to be friendly and loving? It was the one day in the year when people felt drawn more closely together.

"You know," Shirley said after she had been silent for a long while, "you are—lucky, Beverly."

"How do you mean?" Beverly asked smiling.

"Your parents—they worship you," Shirley said slowly.

"And I them," Beverly said promptly.

She knew Shirley's parents were not the sort of parents a girl should have. The Parkers were wealthy, they had money, a lot of it, but their money did not bring their daughter the happy loving home she should have had. They were too busy with their business and social affairs to give Shirley the love and companionship that is every girl's right.

"Their whole world is right in you," Shirley continued.

"That is why it matters so much that I make good at Vernon," Beverly said seriously. "You see, Mother went there, and because of the things she did, the girls made a heroine of her. They expect her daughter to be like her. I can't be other than what my parents expect me to be. They have pinned their hopes on me, and I can't turn out a failure."

"What do they think of your dreams to be a writer?" Shirley asked.

"They want anything that I want," Beverly answered. "If my interests are in writing, they will help me to get that which I want. That is what is so dear about them, they understand me. They never try to force their ideas on me, but accept what I think and help me with the things I do."

"They are two in a hundred," Shirley said shortly. "Not many parents treat their children as really people in their own right. I know mine are as domineering as they can be. I could never love them the way you love yours."

"Perhaps you have never really talked to them about yourself," Beverly said. "Have you ever given them the chance to——"

"I can't keep them to myself for five minutes," Shirley laughed. "I never get the chance to talk seriously to them. You should have heard Mother when I said I wanted to be an actress! 'My deah,' she said, 'really, I don't think you should. Your father has plenty of money, it isn't necessary for you to go on the stage.'"

Beverly laughed, but the next minute she became serious. "Can't you make them see things your way? Can't you make them understand that dramatics mean more to you than society does? After all, there is nothing shameful in a stage career."

"Mother thinks there is," Shirley said miserably. "But I shall keep right on with it, nevertheless. It is the one thing I am really interested in, and I'm not going to give it up! If Mother doesn't come around to my way of thinking, I'm going ahead anyway. She has prevented me from having a lot of things in my life, but I won't lose this. It is my ambition, and I am going to cling to it."

"And I wish you all the success in the world," Beverly declared. "You know, it would be funny, wouldn't it, if we both succeeded in our chosen professions."

"Funny? I don't think so," Shirley declared. "If we work for what we want, and give our best to it, we deserve to succeed. I know I shan't stop until I'm at the top of the ladder."

"You might pass me on the way," Beverly said laughing. "If you do, give me a boost. I shall probably need it."

Shirley laughed. "I'll pull you right along with me."

"You know, writing isn't the easiest profession in the world, and I'm beginning to wonder if I've bitten off more than I can chew."

"What? Beverly Gray getting faint heart?" Shirley scoffed.

"Not exactly," Beverly answered, "but how in the world am I to succeed when there are millions of others trying for the same goal?"

"It might take time, and it will take lots of work," Shirley admitted, "but you will get there. I never saw you start on anything of which you didn't make a success. You have had some writing experience on your high school and the college papers. Now all you have to do is make up your mind what you want to write and stick to it."

"I wish it were as simple as that," Beverly sighed. "In a few months I shall probably throw up the whole thing and get a job as child's nurse."

Shirley laughed. "Not you! You have more determination to stick to one thing than anyone I ever saw. You will be a success, don't doubt that for a minute."

During all these weeks the words Larry had uttered on the last day she saw him had been in her mind: "Some day you will find that love can make up for all the things you think you want now." Could it?

"Shirley——" she began.

"Yes?"

"Suppose you were a great star—a famous stage star. Would you throw up your career for—marriage?"

"I don't know," Shirley said seriously. "I can't tell now, because I'm not famous nor am I in love. If the time ever comes when I have to choose—I don't know what I'll do."

"I don't suppose anyone can tell what one might do," Beverly agreed slowly. "Well, we might as well turn in. Tomorrow is Christmas, and we are going to church early."

When Beverly awoke the next morning snow was drifting down. She jumped from bed and ran across to the window. The world was covered with tiny white crystals. Jack Frost had sketched fantastic pictures on the windows with his icy pen. It was an ideal day to celebrate Christmas. The day of days when everyone should be loving and thoughtful and happy. Beverly whirled back to the bed and pounced on Shirley.

"Wake up, sleepyhead."

"Huh? What's the matter?" Shirley demanded from her cozy posture among the blankets.

"It's snowing!"

"Ooooooo," Shirley snuggled down beneath the covers. "What did you wake me for? I was having the most deli-shi-ous dream."

Beverly bestowed a light kiss on the tip of Shirley's nose and rumpled her friend's hair playfully.

"Come on, get up. It's Christmas."

"Merry Christmas," mumbled Shirley from the depths of the blankets.

"Are you going to get up?" demanded Beverly, her fingers coming in contact with Shirley's ribs.

"Oooo, leggo," Shirley laughed, flinging back the covers and descending on Beverly with a whoop.

Their friendly scrimmage was interrupted by the smiling entrance of Mrs. Gray.

"Breakfast will be ready in a few minutes," she said.

"Righto!" responded Shirley and Beverly breathlessly. "We'll be down in a jiffy."

They hurried through their showers and dressing. When they came to the top of the stairs Beverly stopped and grinned impishly at the banister.

"Doesn't it look tempting?" she murmured mischievously to Shirley.

"Let's do what you are thinking," Shirley laughed.

"Yypee!" trilled Beverly as she slid down the banister. She landed in a heap at her father's feet. Shirley descended on top of her, and there was a mixture of flying legs and arms until Mr. Gray took pity on their muddle and helped them to their feet.

"See here, you wild Indians," he laughed, "that banister wasn't built to stand such punishment."

Beverly giggled. "It will have to stand it with us around."

Mr. Gray put an arm about each girl and drew them toward the dining room. "Come along and eat your breakfast, youngsters. We have to be off for church in a minute."

But breakfast couldn't go uninterrupted—not on Christmas morning. They punctuated their grapefruit and cereal with exclamations of pleased surprise as they divested their Christmas presents of the tissue wrapping and tinsel.

After breakfast they donned hats and coats and walked to church. Everyone in Renville went to church on Christmas morning, and the air was filled with the gay exchange of holiday greetings. The snow still sifted down, covering the earth and people alike with its silvery whiteness. They lifted their strong young contralto voices in Christmas carols in the church sweetly perfumed with frank-incense and myrrh. As they listened to the voice of the minister as he told the old, old story of the greatest love the world has ever known, the meaning of Christmas was borne to them with an ever increasing wonder and reverence.

They walked back to the house slowly in the cold, snowy air.

"This will mean wonderful coasting," Beverly

declared as she laid aside her furs and held out her fingers to the welcome heat of the fire. "Tomorrow we will round up the Lucky Circle and go up to Deacon's Hill."

"How about ice skating?" Shirley asked.

"There is sure to be a lot of that," chimed in Mr. Gray. "We have a lake not far away that will furnish you plenty of ice to skate on."

The snow kept up all afternoon and evening. By the next day, when the party of young people started out with their bob sleds, the snow was feet deep. It was packed down hard on Deacon's Hill, and the sleds flew over the surface with lightning speed. There were tricky curves on the hill, and around these the sleds flashed with a reckless disregard for life and limb.

"Isn't it thrilling?" Beverly demanded as the two climbed onto their sled.

"S'wonderful," admitted Shirley promptly. Her cheeks were red with the sting of the wind, and the air brought a sparkle to her eyes. In her years spent in the city she had never had the chance to enjoy many outdoor sports such as this, and it was new and thrilling.

"Race you," Anne White and Joan Roberts called as they too piled onto their sled.

"It's a go," returned Beverly.

Beverly was first to steer the sled, and Shirley, after giving them a running push to start them, jumped on behind her. For a while they were ahead, and then the other girls' sled began to creep up on them. Inch by inch Anne and Joan gained, until they passed them in a whirl of snow.

"Boo-hoo," murmured Shirley. "They've beaten us."

"Not yet," answered Beverly. "Once we go around the big curve down there we have another chance. The ground is twice as slippery there."

"Cheerio, here we go," sang out Shirley.

The curve was just ahead, and the sled was running swiftly now. As the coasters rounded the bend their horrified gaze saw the two girls and the wrecked sled loom up before them. They were going to crash into them! Shirley, with great presence of mind, threw her arms about Beverly, and together they tumbled from the sled into a snow bank. The sled was empty now and couldn't injure Anne or Joan severely if it crashed into them. A second later they were pulling themselves from the snow bank. Anne and Joan picked themselves up, none the worse for the wreck. A bad accident had been narrowly averted, and all the girls recognized the fact.

"You look like a snow man," laughed Shirley as she helped to brush the snow from Beverly.

"Who wouldn't, after being rolled in it the way we were?" Beverly giggled. "What happened to you two?" she demanded of Anne and Joan. "Don't you know it isn't right to block the traffic that way?"

"The sled struck a snag," Joan explained, "and before we knew it we were on our ear."

"It might have been a bad smash-up if you hadn't dumped from your sled before it hit us," Anne declared.

"Thank Shirley," Beverly said, "she pulled me off before I could even think."

The near-accident had rather spoiled the coasting for the rest of the afternoon, so the Lucky Circle went to Beverly's home and spent the rest of the day singing, dancing, and playing games.

The next day the boys and girls undertook to teach Shirley to ski. Beverly got out her skis and another pair for Shirley, and they joined the rest of the Lucky Circle on Deacon's Hill. Shirley had many spills before she learned to glide smoothly over the snow on the lumbering skis. For three days the Lucky Circle helped her, and soon she began taking long runs down hills. She was beginning to feel the thrill of skiing, the breathless hurtling through space. She was learning to balance herself and didn't feel as tipsy as she had in the beginning.

There were particularly fine places for skiing in the neighborhood, long sloping hills that were free of stumps and snags. The boys and girls whizzed through the air with the grace and ease of young eagles, their arms waving to retain their balance, bodies bent slightly forward.

Shirley, for a moment by herself while the others plunged down the hill, turned from their regular skiing place to a neighboring hill. It was long and looked very inviting. How was it the others avoided this hill? She made up her mind to try it and turned away from her companions. She went skimming over the snow, the wind whistling in her ears and bringing the color to her cheeks. Once she heard Beverly call, and waved a gay hand in response.

"Oh," wailed Beverly, "she will be killed!"

"Not killed," comforted Gordon Brewster, "but she may be badly hurt. That is a big drop."

"Do something," begged Joan Roberts.

The hill Shirley had chosen ended abruptly in a sheer drop of twenty-five feet or more. There had been many accidents there, and now the young people shunned that particular hill, keeping to the safer, if not as thrilling, runway.

"We should have warned her," murmured Anne.

"I never thought she would go there," Beverly declared in a worried voice.

"By a supreme effort she might have cleared the jump," Tommy Chandler suggested.

"She couldn't," declared Barbara West, "she isn't experienced enough on skis."

The seven young people started on a run for the spot where Shirley would be if she had gone over the edge of the cliff. Their skis held them back, and grumbling under their breath because of the delay, they stripped them off impatiently and hurried on. They rounded the edge of the cliff and saw Shirley, a crumpled heap on the white snow.

"Shirley!" Beverly exclaimed.

"Steady!" Boyd Marshall warned. He picked the unconscious girl up in his arms as the others stripped off her skis and started back to Renville with her.

Beverly and Anne ran on ahead. Beverly's mother was out visiting, so the two girls had their hands full with their hasty first-aid preparations. Beverly and Anne put Shirley in bed, and then Anne went down to the living room where the other Lucky Circle members waited in breathless suspense.

"Ooooooo! What a jump!" Shirley murmured painfully when she opened her eyes. She looked up at Beverly and endeavored a grin. "I'll never try that again."

Beverly smiled sympathetically, but her lips trembled. "I hope not. How do you feel?"

"Well," Shirley said a bit dubiously, "I think I am still in one piece. I'll be as fit as a fiddle tomorrow."

"Thank goodness you weren't hurt seriously," Beverly said fervently. "I'd never have forgiven myself if anything happened to you."

"Bosh," Shirley said. "It wasn't your fault I thought I was smarter than I am."

"I should have warned you about that hill," Beverly said. "It is a bad place."

"You're telling me," Shirley murmured.

"Try to sleep," begged Beverly. "It will help you a lot."

"All right," Shirley agreed. "But I warn you, I'm not staying in bed tomorrow. Tomorrow night is the ice-skating party, and I won't miss it for worlds!" Thus she delivered her ultimatum before Beverly drew the shades and left her to herself.

"Well?" the others demanded eagerly as Beverly entered the living room.

"She is all right. She was just shaken up a bit."

"Gosh, we were frightened," Boyd murmured expressively.

Beverly stared reflectively into the fire. "So was I—scared silly. It would have been my fault if anything had happened to her. I never thought to warn her about that cliff."

"Well, all's well that ends well," sighed Joan. "Will she be out for the party tomorrow night?"

Beverly laughed. "We couldn't make her miss it. She has already told me so."

The others took their leave then, and Beverly sneaked a glance in the bedroom at Shirley. She was sleeping peacefully, and Beverly hastily withdrew lest she disturb her. Shirley's fall had affected her quite as much as it had the girl herself. She still felt weak in the knees when she thought of how limp and lifeless Shirley had lain in the snow. It had been so nearly a tragedy! A little harder fall, a little more shock, and Shirley might not be as lively as she was. Fate had been kind, though, and tomorrow Shirley would be none the less active, despite her fall.

After dinner Beverly took a book and settled herself beside Shirley to read aloud.

"I'm making you an awful lot of trouble," Shirley complained, eyes on Beverly and her open book.

"Now who is talking nonsense?" demanded Beverly gently.

"But it must be a lot of bother—serving my dinner to me in bed and now—entertaining me," Shirley insisted.

"But I want to do it," Beverly said innocently.

"You would rather stay here with me than go to the movies with the rest of the Lucky Circle?" Shirley repeated in surprise.

"You are my guest, and more than that—you are my friend," Beverly answered. "If friends can't do little things like this for one another, then they aren't really friends. Besides," she grinned, "when you are in bed I can boss you around."

"Is that so?" Shirley demanded. "Don't get too bossy or I shall come after you."

"You will not," Beverly declared. "You will stay there and listen until I've finished reading."

"I won't listen," Shirley said defiantly, smilingly. "I'll stick my fingers in my ears," she threatened.

"Go right ahead," Beverly invited imperturbably. "I shall go on reading."

Shirley laughed and covered Beverly's hand with her own. "All joking aside, you and your parents have been awfully sweet to me," she said seriously.

"We've loved having you here," Beverly answered. "To me it has been almost like having a sister. I always wanted a sister."

"So did I," Shirley said. "I've nobody to fight with."

Beverly laughed. "It is a good thing we became friends. We are both in the same boat. We can fight with one another."

"That's the trouble," groaned Shirley. "I can't fight with you, because you refuse to quarrel. Every time I get mad about something you merely smile, and then I feel like a silly goose."

Beverly laughed again. "I didn't know I had such control over you. Hereafter I shall proceed to exercise it."

"You influence me enough now," Shirley declared. "You don't have to exert yourself to do it. Every time I go to do anything I think, 'Would Beverly do it? What would she think of it?'"

"It isn't me, it is your conscience," Beverly smiled.

"I never had one until I came to Vernon," continued Shirley. "I never bothered to think what anyone else would do. I did what I wanted to do, never mind what people thought about it. But those days are gone forever. I haven't got any of my impulsiveness any more."

"You have a lot," Beverly answered, "but it is working for your good now. I know and you know that before you came to Vernon you were stubborn and selfish. Now you are a sweet, lovable young lady."

"Whoops! Thanks for them kind words, sister," Shirley giggled. "My, aren't we handing one another flowery compliments tonight? I think we had better stop before we both get conceited over how good we are."

"Perhaps you are right," Beverly agreed, laughing and tossed the book to one side. "Tomorrow the Lucky Circle is going out to the lake to hang lanterns for the party tomorrow night. Will you mind being alone for a few hours?"

"What do you mean 'being alone'?" Shirley demanded quickly. "I'm coming along. Oh, yes, I am," she said as Beverly started to protest. "You can hold forth for hours on how much good it will do me to stay in bed, but I shall finish by going any way, so you might as well save your breath."

"Stubborn!" Beverly said tenderly as she put out the light.

CHAPTER XVII

An Icy Bath

THE NEXT AFTERNOON the Lucky Circle and Shirley started out in an automobile for the lake front to hang Chinese lanterns. Every year during the Christmas holidays the young people of Renville gave a skating party on the lake. It had come to be quite an event, and was looked forward to by young and old skaters as well. Refreshments—hot chocolate and frankfurters—were served. A big fire was built in an open stone fireplace, and over this the "dogs" were roasted and the chocolate heated. This year the young people were looking forward to a particularly bright occasion. The cold weather had frozen the lake over thickly, and it was ideal for skating.

The boys strung wires along the edge of the lake front, and on these the girls hung gay Chinese lanterns. The boys started out then to inspect the ice, placing warning signs near the spots that were thin. The girls gathered sticks from the woods near by and stacked them high near the open fireplace.

It was late in the afternoon before they were finished and piled into the automobile once more to drive back to their homes for supper. The open air had given each one a ravenous appetite.

"Gosh," Shirley declared after dinner, "I've never eaten so much before! It's a good thing I don't live hereabouts, the air makes me too hungry. I would soon be able to get a job as the fat lady in the circus."

After dinner Beverly and Shirley and Mr. and Mrs. Gray got their skates and piled into the Gray automobile. It was a fifteen-minute drive to the lake front, and they covered it in record time. The rest of the Lucky Circle had already arrived, and they greeted Beverly and Shirley with shouts. There was a crowd of people gathered putting on skates, and some were already skimming over the ice.

"Hello, Miss Beverly," a chubby little fellow grinned up at Beverly.

"Hello, Bucky," the girl answered smiling. "I haven't seen you since I've been home."

"No'm, I been sick."

"Oh, that's too bad," Beverly said quickly.

"No, 'tain't," he grinned. "I ain't been ta school for a week."

"Oh, don't you like school?" Beverly asked.

"Oh, it's all right," he said unenthusiastically, "but our teacher asks the funniest questions. I had a hot dog already," he volunteered. "Miss Barbara gave it to me."

"She did!" Beverly exclaimed. "Do you think she would give me one?"

"I don't know," he frowned. "I lit the fire for her, maybe that had something to do with it."

"Maybe it did," Beverly laughed. "That is Bucky Harris," Beverly said to Shirley as the little fellow moved away. "He lives across the street from us."

"Lively, isn't he?" Shirley smiled.

"And as full of mischief as they come," Beverly answered. "He is a good skater, too, for such a youngster."

Beverly and Shirley swung out on the ice together. They skimmed along, their cheeks red and eyes dancing from the biting tang in the air. Overhead the gay lanterns lent an air of festivity to the usually barren shore. Nearly all the people in Renville who owned skates or cared in any way for the sport were out tonight. Old and young alike were there to join in the fun.

Beverly was called away for a moment, and Shirley found herself alone, but not for long.

"Hello!" said little Bucky Harris.

"Hello!" responded Shirley with a smile.

"What's your name?" inquired the youngster.

"Shirley."

"Mine's Bucky. Are you a friend of Beverly?" he wanted to know.

"I room with her at college," the girl answered.

"I'm going to college when I get big," he declared. "I'm going to be on the football team, and the baseball team, and study to be a doctor."

"That will be fine," Shirley declared. "Do you like doctors?"

"No," he answered truthfully. "But I'm goin' to be different than most doctors. I'll never give people medicine that tastes bad."

"I take it you had some medicine that didn't taste good," Shirley laughed.

"Oh, it was terrible stuff," he declared. "What's going to happen now?"

"They are going to have a race," answered Shirley.

Boyd and Gordon were marking off the starting and finishing points, and the young people were lining up.

"Come on, Shirley," Beverly called. "We want to get in this."

One of the older people acted as the judge and gave the signal for the start. The skates flashed like silver over the ice as one after the other the boys and girls sped away from the starting line. There were girls there who were as efficient skaters as the boys, but it soon developed who the best skaters were. Tommy Chandler and Gordon Brewster began to pull ahead of the others, each boy doing his level best to beat the other to the finish line. Cheers of encouragement urged them on. For the three-minutes' time during which they strove to beat each other they were friendly enemies, and the boys flung quips back and forth. Inch by inch Gordon forged ahead. It looked as though Tommy had no chance of winning, when with a final spurt of speed and determination he began to close the distance between himself and his friend. Gordon was giving all he had, but Tommy kept coming until he was even with Gordon and then past him.

Tommy won and was congratulated on all hands.

"Swell skating, old top," Gordon declared. He had lost, but he was a good sport. He was quite satisfied with having done his best.

"Thanks," Tommy said.

"Ladies and gentlemen—the winnah!" Boyd

raised Tommy's hand above his head in a token of victory.

"What's next on the program?" Tommy demanded.

"It seems," Boyd said ponderously, "that there are some fancy skaters in dear old Renville."

"Who would have thought it?" murmured Barbara.

"Exactly," said Boyd. "However, these fancy skaters have declared themselves more than willing to grace the evening by performing some of their peculiar antics."

"Are they graceful?" inquired Joan innocently.

"They had better be," answered Boyd frowning, "or else——"

"Hush, here they come," murmured Anne.

A young man and girl swung out on the ice. They had donned fancy costumes for the occasion, and the colored lanterns overhead shed gay colors over them. Gracefully and artfully they swung through their difficult, intricate steps. Someone had turned on a car radio and the music filtered down to the group on the ice. It was like a story-book scene: two fancy skaters beneath the glowing lights, keeping time with their steps and movements to the music that was wafted to them on the faint breeze. The sweaters and caps of the other skaters were spots of color on the ice and at one side the fire in the open fireplace roared high. When the exhibition came to an end, the audience overwhelmed the skaters with applause.

Then general skating began again. The Lucky Circle joined hands, and in the long line they formed sped in and out between the others. Finally they paired off, and two by two they skated and cut figures.

Boyd and Shirley stopped at one side of the lake to rest and to watch.

"Would you like a hot dog?" Boyd asked.

"I certainly would," Shirley declared.

He grinned. "You and me both. Wait a minute and I'll be back with some."

He sped away over the ice to the open fireplace, and Shirley waited alone. To one side, and rather far out on the ice near the middle of the lake, was little Bucky Harris. He was an amusing youngster and quite talkative. He saw her and waved a gay hand. He was skating near thin ice, and she motioned him to keep away. Evidently he misunderstood her and kept on. A minute more, and the thin ice had broken beneath his feet. The little fellow was plunged into the icy water.

Shirley looked wildly about for help. She was nearest, and she sped forward. She had to reach him before he went down! Head down, breath coming in great gasps, she flew over the ice. By now more skaters had seen the unfortunate Bucky and were speeding to the scene, but Shirley was far ahead of them. Bucky had been farther out than she had thought. What had possessed him to go so far away from the other skaters? She had better be careful. The ice out here wasn't too thick, and it would soon break beneath her weight. She slowed her pace, and within a few feet of the hole in the ice through which Bucky had disappeared, got down on her knees. Carefully she crawled toward the hole. Bucky was holding onto the edge of the ice, his little face and hands already blue with the cold. She reached out. A few inches more and she could grasp his hand.

She crept a few inches nearer. The warning crack of the ice echoed in her ears, and she drew back hastily but not soon enough. In a minute she was plunged head first into the icy, black water beside Bucky. A scream rose from the other skaters as the water closed over Shirley. In a moment she came to the surface, gasping for breath. Bucky had gone under again, and she dove for him. When she came up she had Bucky in her arms. The little fellow was all in. And no wonder! Her teeth were chattering. The water was unbelievably cold! Skaters were drawing nearer, but she motioned them back, shouting a warning. How were the rescuers to get to them with the ice crumbling under the slightest pressure? Whenever she grasped the raw edges to pull herself up, the ice broke away in her hands. Bucky and the weight of her wet clothes were pulling her down. The rescuers had to reach them soon! Not for her own sake alone, but for the sake of the little boy. He was all tired out and chilled to the bone. She tried to lift Bucky, but he was a dead weight in her arms.

"Bucky!" She shook him roughly to rouse him.

He shook the water from his eyes and endeavored a grin, though his lips were blue with the cold.

"Brave boy," she murmured. "I'm going to try to lift you onto the ice. When you can, creep away from the hole as fast as you are able. Understand? Do you understand?" she asked, shaking him again.

"S-s-sure," he shivered.

"Here we go now." She grasped him by the knees, and he tried to pull himself up on the ice. "Keep trying," she directed when he would have stopped. "You'll make it!"

Little by little and with her help he pulled himself out. Inch by inch he crept away from the yawning hole. Shirley sank back, and the dark water closed over her head. At least she had saved him. She came to the surface gasping. The water had a hideous taste, and she hadn't meant to swallow so much of it. Bucky was crawling toward the other skaters, who were watching fearfully lest the ice should break beneath him. He reached the crowd of skaters and was lifted into loving arms while a shout went up from hoarse throats. Boys and men were still endeavoring to reach Shirley by crawling to the hole from different directions, but the warning crack, crack of the ice sent them scurrying back.

The girl in the water was half frozen. Her clothes felt like ice packs clinging to her body. She was cold to the very marrow of her bones. Her teeth chattered continuously, and her arms and legs felt like sticks. They refused to bear her up any longer or to respond to the urgency she put on them. Why continue to fight? It was so much easier to sink and let the water lull the thought of the cold from her mind. But Shirley fought to the surface once more. Something struck her across the shoulder, and a voice, urgent and beseeching, came to her ears:

"Shirley! Grasp the rope! Catch it! Hold on—tight!"

It was Beverly's voice. She and the Lucky Circle had found a rope and tossed one end to Shirley. Obedient to her friend's voice she caught the rough rope in her fingers. Wonderful girl—Beverly. Beverly said to hold on, and she endeavored to do so. But it was no use. Her nerveless grasp slid from the rope, and her head sank beneath the water again. She came to the surface once more and filled her lungs with the air. It was getting more and more difficult to come up when she was dragged down.

"Shirley! The rope—catch it! You've got to hang on!"

Beverly again. The rope spun across the water, and in response to the urgency in her friend's voice Shirley caught hold of it. The young people on the other end began to pull, and little by little Shirley felt herself being lifted clear of that dreadful, chilling water. She was almost clear when the ice crumpled beneath her and her fingers slid from the rope. A groan went up from the crowd breathlessly watching as she went below the surface. Somehow it seemed as if the water just wouldn't let her go. She was beginning to lose consciousness, and she recognized the fact. The cold was getting too much for her. In another minute she would go down not to come up again.

"But, Beverly, you can't do it!" Anne pleaded.

"I can, too," Beverly declared. "If the ice breaks under me, you can pull me out. I tell you, it is the only chance."

"I think you are right," Boyd admitted, "but let me go."

Beverly shook her head. "I don't weigh as much as you. The ice might hold me."

She tied the rope securely about her waist and started out. Her idea was that she might be able to get close enough to grasp hold of Shirley. If she too fell into the water, she would have the rope already secure about her waist and her friends could haul her out—with Shirley. She had to reach Shirley! The girl was half frozen now, and it was a miracle that she had been able to hold herself above water so long.

Beverly crept out onto the perilous ice, the rope dragging across the white expanse behind her. The ice cracked warningly beneath her, but she kept on. None of the men or boys could have gotten this close to the hole in the ice. The ice was too thin, and they were too heavy. They would have been plunged beneath the surface long before this. Inch by inch she was nearing the hole that held Shirley. She caught a glimpse of the girl's white face. Shirley's eyes were closed, and a cold fear caught at Beverly's heart. It couldn't be! Shirley was strong and healthy—but she had been in the icy water for a long while. She had done a brave thing when she plunged in after little Bucky. Beverly had to go slowly and carefully, but in the end her cautiousness went for naught. The ice cracked beneath her, and she was hurled into the cold, dark water. She went under and came up spluttering. The water was horribly cold. Already she was shivering. She glanced around and quickly swam toward Shirley. The girl was unconscious, and no wonder! How she had managed to fight the coldness as long as she had was a mystery to Beverly.

Beverly signaled her friends to pull them clear of the water, and the Lucky Circle responded with vigor. Beverly grasped Shirley under the arms and held her up. The boys and girls pulled the two from the water and onto the ice. Beverly endeavored to lift Shirley to bear her across the ice, but she could not. The water-laden clothes and the cold had weakened her, and she could scarcely stand by herself.

Reckless of the fact that the ice might crack any minute and plunge them all into the freezing water, the Lucky Circle rushed out and helped the two survivors back to the shore. Blankets were wrapped about them, and Beverly and the unconscious Shirley were put into the Gray machine and hastily borne back to the Gray home. Mr. and Mrs. Gray had stood in frightened, breathless suspense as they watched their daughter risk her own life to rescue Shirley. Now they too raced against time to save

Shirley's life. Unless she received proper attention promptly, pneumonia might develop from her experience.

Shirley came to herself as they bore her into the house and put her between warm blankets. She was seized with a fit of shivering that shook her from head to foot. Beverly had changed into dry clothes, and now she helped her mother do what she could until the doctor arrived. When the doctor had given his orders and they had been followed to the letter, Mrs. Gray fed them both hot drinks and tucked them in warm beds. Long into the night Shirley continued to be attacked by those racking fits of trembling. They had done all they could to ward off any serious effects of her icy bath, and now they could do nothing but wait for the shivering to pass. For hours her teeth chattered, and her hands were as cold as ice to the touch.

In the morning when Beverly awoke, Shirley was already awake. As a result of her freezing plunge, she suffered a heavy cold, and it was noticeable the minute she talked. Beverly herself had a slight attack of the sniffles, but not enough to keep her in bed. The doctor came again in the morning and prescribed several days in bed for Shirley, in addition to medicine that was particularly difficult to swallow.

"Oooo, that's awful stuff!" Shirley grimaced as Mrs. Gray gave her a dose of the doctor's prescription.

Beverly giggled unfeelingly. "You shouldn't go swimming in the winter time."

"You shouldn't laugh," Mrs. Gray said, smiling. "You have to take some too."

"Oh," Beverly wailed, "it is Shirley who has the cold."

"The doctor said to give it to you, too, so you don't get one," her mother declared.

"Ha, ha!" giggled Shirley at Beverly's wry face. " 'He who laughs last——' " she quoted.

"Is there anything special you would like to have for lunch?" Mrs. Gray asked.

When Beverly and Shirley had given this important detail the proper amount of consideration, Mrs. Gray departed, and the girls settled down to a game of checkers. They played one game after another, until both declared themselves disgusted with the sight of the checkerboard. Next they worked jigsaw and cross-word puzzles, but time dragged along. In the afternoon a diversion was created in the form of six Lucky Circle members who descended on the two with shouts of laughter and gay raillery.

"Shirley, my girl, you are a heroine," Anne informed her friend.

Shirley laughed. "Where's my medal?"

"No fooling," the others chimed in. "Everybody is talking about how brave it was for you to dive into the water after Bucky."

"I didn't dive," Shirley contradicted smilingly, "I fell."

"Did she fall or was she pushed?" Boyd chirped.

"Nevertheless," Joan insisted, "it was brave of you."

"What about Beverly?" Shirley demanded. "She dived in after me."

"Oh, well, we've always known Beverly was brave," Tommy declared, laughing.

"Please!" Beverly giggled. "My modesty!"

"You know," Boyd said thoughtfully, "it is strange, but no one ever gave me a medal for my brave deeds. I can't understand why."

The others roared.

"Brave deeds!" Joan mocked. "And what might I ask do you consider a brave deed?"

"Um—oh—I can't recall them offhand," Boyd grinned.

"That's because there aren't any to recall," Gordon declared.

"There are, too. Didn't I rescue a cat from the

top of a tree last year?" Boyd demanded indignantly.

"Such heroism," Joan murmured.

"What else?" Barbara asked.

"Uh—er—I'll let you guess the rest of them," Boyd declared.

"We never guess," Joan interrupted. "You have to show us."

"You just don't appreciate me," wailed Boyd tearfully. "You don't know a brave man when you see one."

"Sure we do," Gordon acknowledged. "Where is he?"

Thereafter ensued another one of the teasing arguments between the boys and girls. The Lucky Circle were all jolly young people, and they kept up the merriment far into the afternoon. They hurled teasing quips back and forth with a reckless abandon for feelings. Of course, each one recognized what was said was meant only in fun. None of them could take offense at the mischievous remarks.

"Hear, hear!" Boyd interrupted the levity. "I have a proposition to make."

"It better be good," warned Tommy.

"It is," solemnly assured Boyd.

"Let's hear it," Joan suggested.

"I propose——" Boyd began.

"Yes, yes, do go on," urged Barbara.

"That we make Shirley Parker an honorary member of the Lucky Circle." Boyd looked about at the smiling faces of the other members. "All in favor say 'aye.'"

A loud chorus of "Ayes" almost overwhelmed him. He beamed on Shirley. "I hereby initiate you into the deep and dark secrets of our most august organization."

"I must say I am truly honored," declared Shirley, the color rising to her cheeks. "I'm more than proud to be considered worthy of becoming one of your members."

"That calls for a celebration," Beverly decided. "I think Mother has some sandwiches and chocolate just longing to be devoured by eight ravenous people."

"Lead me to 'em," Boyd pleaded dramatically. "It is just the sort of nourishment I am in need of at this moment."

"As though you didn't eat 'em at any moment," scoffed Gordon.

"Sir, I'll have you know——" Boyd was beginning indignantly when Mrs. Gray's entrance interrupted him.

"Here is another visitor for you, Shirley," Mrs.

Gray said as she entered bearing a tray of sandwiches and hot chocolate. "Bucky is here to see you."

"Hello!" said that youngster appearing in the doorway.

"Well, Bucky," Boyd beamed, "I thought you would be in bed after your bath last night."

"Naw," the little fellow grinned, "I been in the water more than once."

"What is the idea of the fishing pole?" Gordon demanded.

The little boy was clasping a long, slender, bamboo fishing pole in his cherubic fist.

"It's for Miss Shirley," he answered solemnly.

"For me?" Shirley murmured in surprise.

"Yes'm."

"But why?" Shirley asked.

" 'Cause you pulled me out of the water last night. It is my best one," he continued. "I want ta give it to you—fer rescuin' me."

Shirley recognized the generous impulse that had prompted the little fellow to part with his best fishing pole, and she didn't want to hurt his feelings by refusing it, but she couldn't really see what she could do with a fishing pole at Vernon.

"Thanks, Bucky," she said smiling. "I appreciate

it very much, but I don't see how I could get it in my suitcase to take back to school with me."

"That's so," he agreed seriously. "Perhaps you better carry it so."

"Or better still," Shirley said quickly, "why don't you keep it for me until I come to Renville again? There is no place to fish about the school. So you keep it here with you until I get another chance to come to visit Beverly, and then you can take me fishing with you."

"All right," the little fellow agreed. "Will you mind if I use it now and then?"

"Not at all," Shirley said magnanimously. "Use it all you like—just as if you hadn't given it to me at all."

"Have a sandwich, Bucky?" Boyd interrupted.

Thereafter Bucky entertained the eight others with his funny comments, and when it was time for the others to depart he went along with them, his fishing pole still tightly clasped in his hand. Evidently it was a big relief to him that he didn't have to part with this, his most prized possession.

The girls spent another quiet evening reading and talking together. The next day both colds were greatly improved. By the time the day dawned when they were to start back to Vernon, they were their old healthy selves again.

"I certainly won't forget this visit," Shirley declared when they were packing. "I've had the most fun I ever had during Christmas holidays."

"Then you will come again soon?" Beverly asked, sitting on her suitcase to close it.

"I shouldn't be surprised if I came so often you had to tell me to stay away," Shirley declared, laughing.

CHAPTER XVIII

Hamlet

" 'To be or not to be, that is the question,' " quoted Shirley, pacing back and forth in her room, waving the script of the play dramatically in the air.

" 'Sterrible," Lenora declared bluntly.

"Oh, yeah?" Shirley demanded slangily and continued imperturbably: " 'Whether 'tis—whether 'tis——' "

"Nobler," supplied Lois.

" 'Whether 'tis nobler in the—in the——' "

"Mind," suggested Lenora. "Something very few people possess."

"Did you look at me when you said that?" demanded Lois.

Lenora giggled. "I didn't, but since you admit that I'm right——"

"I admitted no such thing!" Lois said loudly. "I——"

"End of round one!" Beverly called.

The Christmas holidays were weeks past, and the school term had begun again with its rounds of studies and extra-curricular activities. The girls were together again, and the chatter and teasing flew back and forth as thickly as ever.

The junior class was to give Shakespeare's immortal play *Hamlet* in April. Lenora had been appointed stage director, manager, and what have you, just as she had directed *Romeo and Juliet* during the girls' freshman year. Shirley was to play the leading rôle of Hamlet, and Lois, much against her will, was cast as the lovely Ophelia. Of course, there were more characters than these two in the play, and they had been chosen with great care from the ranks of the junior class by Lenora. Beverly had firmly declined to play the Queen. The others had coaxed and pleaded with her to accept the rôle, but she remained firm, with the declaration that she would be sure to get stage-struck. She knew her capabilities, and they did not include acting. She had accepted the post in charge of the scenery, and had chosen Anne as her assistant. Rosalie had charge of the costumes, and so it was that all the Alphas, in some way or another, were connected with the production.

This afternoon the girls had received their parts,

and Shirley and Lois, under Lenora's direction, were going over the lines in Beverly's and Shirley's room in Chadwick Hall. Beverly was an amused spectator at this first attempt to act *Hamlet*. At the rate Shirley and Lois were progressing, it threatened to be a comedy instead of the tragedy it should be.

" 'To sleep! perchance to dream! ay, there's the rub,' " continued Shirley, consulting her script.

"You don't say that right," Lenora pointed out. "Say it like this, 'ay, there's the rub!' "

Shirley shook her head undecidedly. "I wonder if I shall learn it."

"Wait until we start regular rehearsals," predicted Lois.

"Yes, just wait," seconded Lenora. "It threatens to be worse than *Romeo and Juliet* was."

"That wasn't so bad," defended Lois. "Shirley had the chance of becoming a real stage star because of her acting in that play."

It was true. A New York producer of theatrical plays had seen the freshman production of *Romeo and Juliet,* and after the final curtain he had come around to the dressing room to see Shirley. He had offered her a chance to play Juliet in his production in his theater in New York, but she had declined, much to the astonishment of her friends.

She had no desire to go into actual theater work until after her graduation from Vernon.

"You won't win anything for this production," predicted Lenora firmly. "*Hamlet* is always a hard tragedy to play."

"With you for our director it is a tragedy already," Lois said daringly, teasingly.

Lenora quelled her boisterous friend with an unoffending pillow and turned back to Shirley.

"Let's hear you say that again."

Obediently Shirley continued with Hamlet's speech.

"You've got to be good in this," Lois declared to Shirley. "May Norris almost murdered Lenora because she didn't get the part."

May Norris was a junior and no friend of any of the Alphas. Last term Shirley had been on the verge of being expelled for something May had done, when the real culprit was discovered. Ever since then May had taken a violent dislike to all of the Alpha girls. She too was interested in dramatics and had her heart set on playing the lead in this term's production. But because of Shirley's success in the first year's play, the part had gone to her, and May was jealous. She would do anything she could to keep Shirley from playing the part on the opening night.

"I finally consented to let her be Shirley's understudy," Lenora said. "I had to declare peace some way."

"That means, if anything happens to Shirley, that May will have the leading part on opening night, doesn't it?" Lois demanded.

"Yes," Lenora admitted, "as much as I hate it, that is what will happen."

"Then take care, Shirley," Lois advised. "May would do anything to get you out of the way."

"I don't think she would stoop to foul play," Beverly put in. "May might be jealous and all that, but she wouldn't do anything to actually harm Shirley."

"Wouldn't she though," Lenora laughed. "She was willing that Shirley should be expelled in her place last term, wasn't she?"

"But she has changed," Beverly said again.

"No, she hasn't," Lois declared. "Beverly, you are too easy. You forgive too easily. May has no love for you either. How can you speak well of her?"

"If I can't speak good of her, I won't speak ill," Beverly said promptly. "I'm not perfect myself, why should I criticize her?"

"I know what you mean," Lois said, flushing. "You are telling me that people who live in glass houses shouldn't throw stones. I suppose I have plenty of faults of my own."

"As Shakespeare said," quoted Lenora, " 'take each man's censure, but reserve thy judgment.' "

"Exactly," Shirley said. "I don't think May would do anything, either. She will just have to remain my understudy, for I am going to play the leading rôle when we give the play."

"You bet you are!" added Lenora. "You are Vernon's original star, and the play won't go on without you."

During the days that followed, the girls started regular rehearsals. Each member of the cast was working hard to make this play a success. It was hard for amateurs to acquire the poise of experienced actors, but little by little they were doing it. Lenora, as director, kept them working at their parts day after day until even she began to think they were getting good.

May Norris seemed quite content with her part as Shirley's understudy, and the girls began to think they had been wrong about her. Then one afternoon something happened that brought back all their former suspicions.

"Shirley, go to the storeroom and get that saber you are supposed to wear," directed Lenora.

"Righto," responded Shirley and departed.

The storeroom was in the basement of the auditorium, and in it the dramatic societies kept a supply of costumes.

"Hi, Shirley, where goest thou?" demanded a gay voice.

Shirley turned to greet Josephine Carter, another junior, who was to play the part of the Queen in the play.

"Hello, I'm going down to the storeroom," Shirley answered. "I've got to find the saber that goes with my costume."

"I know where it is," Josephine volunteered. "I'll get it. I have to get my costume, too."

"Thanks," Shirley said, promptly accepting her offer. "Bring it out to the stage when you come up, will you?"

"Sure."

Shirley turned to make her way back to the rehearsal stage when a scream rang out behind her. Immediately she ran back to the storeroom from whence the scream had emanated.

The stairs leading to the basement were in total darkness, and Shirley picked her way carefully down them.

"Who screamed?" she demanded as she reached the basement floor.

Groans came from the storeroom, and Shirley turned in that direction. There was a short flight of steps leading into the storeroom which was on a lower level than the basement. These steps too were in darkness, and Shirley stumbled badly as she went down them. She remembered there was a flashlight on a shelf in the storeroom, and she felt her way to it. Finding it, she switched it on and flashed the light about the storeroom. Josephine Carter lay in a heap to one side of the stairs. Shirley rushed to her and helped the girl to rise.

The other girls, who had been out in front of the auditorium on the stage, had heard the scream, and now they arrived, breathless and excited, on the scene.

"What happened?" Lenora demanded. "What's wrong?"

"It's my arm," Josephine groaned.

"She slipped and fell down the steps," Shirley explained.

"Slipped nothing," Josephine said quickly. "Somebody pushed me."

"Nonsense," Lenora said crisply. "Who would want to push you and why?"

"Just the same, someone did," the girl maintained. "The lights wouldn't work, so I came down in the dark after the flashlight, and just as I got to the top of the steps here leading down into the storeroom someone gave me a shove from behind."

"What's the matter with your arm?" Lenora asked.

"I—I think it is broken," Josephine answered, her face white with pain.

"Come on, we'll take you to the infirmary and have the doctor look at it," Shirley said quickly.

"This is a fine how-de-do," Lenora groaned, sinking down on Beverly's bed. "What are we going to do now?"

Rehearsals had been abandoned when Josephine met with her accident and the girls had taken her to the college infirmary. Afterward the six Alphas had come back to their usual spot in Chadwick Hall.

"With Josephine's arm broken, who is going to play the part of the Queen?" the director continued.

"And we have only two weeks for rehearsals, too," Lois added gloomily.

"Something like this would have to happen," Rosalie said pessimistically.

"Do you really think someone pushed her down the steps?" Anne asked.

"Who would do such a thing?" Beverly scoffed.

"I think she dreamed it," Shirley laughed.

"Just a minute!" Lenora jumped up suddenly, snapping her fingers. "I've got it."

"So what?" Lois drawled.

"I understand now," Lenora said excitedly. "Somebody did push Josephine down those stairs."

"What makes you say that?" asked Beverly.

"I sent Shirley down to the storeroom, didn't I?" Lenora demanded.

"Well," Lois said slowly, "maybe I'm dumb, but I don't see——"

"Wait a minute," Lenora continued. "I sent Shirley down to the storeroom. May Norris was on the stage and heard me tell Shirley to get the saber."

"And she left the stage right after Shirley did," Lois added, beginning to see Lenora's meaning.

"You mean that May Norris pushed Josephine down the steps in the dark?" Rosalie asked.

"She pushed Josephine," Lenora nodded, "but she didn't know it was Josephine."

"I don't understand," Anne frowned.

"Nor I," said Shirley.

"Oh, don't you see?" Lenora said impatiently. "She waited until she thought Shirley was on her way to the storeroom. May slipped into the basement after her. In the darkness she could not see that the girl she pushed wasn't Shirley, but Josephine."

"You mean that it was her idea to push me down the steps?" Shirley demanded.

"Of course," finished Lois. "If you twisted your ankle, or broke your arm, as Josephine did, you couldn't play Hamlet, and that would give May her big chance."

"It's perfectly plain," Lenora added.

Shirley shook her head. "That seems like a dirty trick. I wouldn't believe even May would do that."

"She did do it," Lenora insisted. "Everything fits together like pieces of a puzzle."

"I wouldn't spread word of this about the campus," Beverly advised. "You know we can't be sure, and it wouldn't do to accuse the girl of such a thing."

"No," Shirley agreed. "We better say no more about it."

"Meanwhile," Lenora groaned, "we are still out of a Queen."

"Who in the world will we get to take the part?" Lois demanded.

Lenora cocked a speculative eye in Rosalie's direction. "Will you?"

"No," exploded Rosalie. "I couldn't play the Queen, I'm not the type at all."

Anne next came in for Lenora's regard, but she too declined with vigor. Lenora then passed on to Beverly.

"You'll have to do it, Beverly."

"Oh, no," Beverly laughed. "I'm not an actress."

"Oh, come on, Beverly, be a sport. You wouldn't want the play to be a flop, would you?" Lois persuaded.

"Of course not."

"Then play the part of the Queen," Lenora pleaded. "You are the only one who could do it, it is such short notice. All the other girls would fall down on it."

"How do you know I wouldn't?" Beverly demanded. "I've never played before a really big audience."

"You could do it, I know you could," Lenora declared. "Will you?"

"But——" Beverly began laughingly.

"Come on, Beverly," Shirley urged. "It isn't exactly a leading part, and you could play it."

"Sure you could," Anne chimed in.

"It's up to you whether we give the play or not," Lenora said finally. "You've been to rehearsals and practically know the part already. There is no time to break in a new player. You've got to do it."

"Well," Beverly conceded slowly, "if I make a

mess of things, remember you brought it on yourself."

"You won't fail us," Lenora said confidently.

"I hope not," Beverly said, but not in the least
bit confidently.

CHAPTER XIX

An Understudy Triumphs

FROM THAT DAY ON Beverly played the part of the Queen, in addition to her other duties of arranging the scenery. Rehearsals went forward as per schedule, and the play was to be given on the second Saturday in April. That left two weeks for everything to be attended to. Tickets were proclaimed on sale, and they sold swiftly. Friends, relatives, students, and faculty members all desired to be present at this the second play to be produced by the same brilliant cast as had given *Romeo and Juliet* two years ago.

The two weeks went by swiftly, almost too swiftly. The cast was becoming nervous, and Lenora was at her wit's end with last-minute details. Shirley coached Beverly for her part and was sure Beverly could make a hit of it, but Beverly herself was uncertain. She had been in high-school theatricals and church productions, but she had never played before a really big audience.

May Norris, observed wonderingly by the Alpha members, was making a definite bid for Shirley's friendship. None of the six had mentioned their suspicion that she had pushed Josephine down the storeroom steps, and evidently no one else had such a thought, for nothing ever came to light about the "accident." But what could be her idea in becoming friends with Shirley? Shirley herself thought the girl had had a change of heart, so Shirley was friendly with her. Lenora and Lois, however, were inclined to be suspicious. May Norris had never been friendly with any of them before, and they distrusted her now. Did she think in some way she could manage to play the leading rôle on opening night? If so, the girls vowed, she was doomed for a disappointment. Nothing, Lenora declared fervently, would induce her to let May play Hamlet in Shirley's place. However, they refused to worry about possibilities now; they had their hands full as it was.

"Don't be nervous," Shirley said consolingly, "just forget all about the audience."

"I wish I could," Beverly wailed. "I just know something will go wrong!"

"Nonsense," Lenora said crisply. "Everybody.

that will be here is your friend. They want to see you make a success of it. Remember that, and you won't let them scare you."

"Just the same," Beverly said, "I'll have to face them and—what if I should forget my lines?"

"You can think of more depressing things than anyone I know of," Lois declared. "It isn't like you, Beverly, to be pessimistic."

"I'm not used to acting, either," Beverly retorted. "I'd do anything but this."

"Well," Lenora said brightly, "you can't leave us flat now. You have to go through with it, and you better be good."

"Yes, ma'am," said Beverly meekly.

"You too, Lois," Lenora said frowning. "As Ophelia you are terrible. Ophelia was graceful, but you——"

"How can anyone be graceful in such flowing robes?" Lois demanded. "I expect any minute to trip and fall flat."

Shirley and Beverly laughed. The picture of Lois falling flat on the stage was too much for their sense of humor. If such a thing happened on Saturday night, the audience would howl with laughter. The play hadn't much chance of being a real tragedy.

"If any of you dare to fall down on your parts,"

Lenora threatened, "after all the work we've had getting ready——"

"We won't," Shirley assured her between giggles, "We really know our parts; there is nothing to worry about."

"Nothing to worry about?" bellowed Lenora. "I shan't sleep a wink until the thing is over."

"Let's call rehearsal off and go down to Weller's," Lois suggested. "I'm tired."

"Not any more so than the rest of us," retorted Lenora, "but we aren't leaving here until we go through that second scene again. Do you realize the play is to be given tomorrow night?"

"We realize it all right," said Beverly, "and personally, I'm shaking in my boots."

"You will get over it," Lenora said. "Now let's see that scene again."

Patiently, resignedly, the players went through their parts. Lenora made several changes, and they went through it once more. Finally she decided it was all right, and everyone declared the rehearsal over. They would rehearse again tomorrow morning. It would be the last dress rehearsal before the time when the play was to be given. Any last minute changes that were absolutely necessary could be made then.

Cheerfully the girls left the auditorium for Wel-

ler's. They had a little time before dinner at the
Hall, and they journeyed to the soda emporium to
enjoy themselves.

The following morning dawned cool and clear.
It gave promise of a wonderful night on which to
give their play. It being Saturday, the girls lingered
over their breakfast, discussing the latest campus
news.

After breakfast, the cast of *Hamlet* assembled in
the living room and directed their steps toward the
auditorium for their last dress rehearsal. They
donned their costumes and for hours rehearsed
scene after scene. But Lenora was a hard taskmas-
ter. Their plays were always a success because she,
as director, insisted on everything being as nearly
perfect as possible. No halfway measures for her.
The girls would work until she was satisfied, or
they wouldn't produce the play at all. The girls
coöperated marvelously and accepted all her criti-
cisms and rebukes meekly. Lenora knew more
about coaching a play than any of them, so they
offered her no argument.

They went back to Chadwick Hall for
luncheon. They were returning to the auditorium
for minor touches to the play when Shirley discovered that she had left her copy of the script at
the Hall.

"Go along to the auditorium," she proposed. "I'll catch up with you."

"Righto," Lenora said, "but hurry. We want to get this over with."

"Be with you in a jiffy," Shirley promised.

Shirley turned back to the Hall to find her script. She had had it in the living room before lunch. It was there she looked first. Then she went up to her room and turned everything upside down in her haste. The script was nowhere to be found. She went back to the living room. It must be here. She had left it on the little table there beside the chair where she had been sitting.

"Hello, Shirley. Is this what you are looking for?" May Norris inquired sweetly, helpfully holding out the lost script.

"Yes, thanks," Shirley said. She had been as surprised as the other girls when May Norris became friendly toward her, but she had accepted the girl's obvious sincerity as genuine. "Where did you find it?"

"On the floor," May answered. "It must have fallen from the table."

"I suppose it did," Shirley answered and turned to go.

"Wait a minute," May called, accompanying her to the door. "Do you have rehearsal again?"

"Just the last scene. There are some minute changes Lenora wants to make. You are my understudy, you better come along," Shirley said.

May laughed. "There is not much chance of my having to play the part, so I won't bother. Have you heard the latest news?"

"What is that?" Shirley asked interestedly.

"Mysterious lights and figures have been seen in the old Horler Mansion again."

Last term the girls had had some exciting adventures in the old Horler Mansion, when skeletons and ghosts who were supposed to haunt the place had turned out to be smugglers. It was through their interest in the smugglers that the girls had met Larry Owens. He had been the Secret Service agent on the trail of the law breakers.

"Is that so?" Shirley asked excitedly. "When were they seen?"

"Last night and night before last," May answered. "Let's go out there and see if we can find some of the ghosts," she proposed in a whisper.

"I can't," Shirley said reluctantly. "It is important that I rehearse this last scene for Lenora."

"It won't take long," May urged. "We can be back inside an hour."

"I'd like to," Shirley said, "but——"

"What is the matter? Are you afraid of the ghosts?" May demanded, smiling.

"Of course I'm not afraid," Shirley bristled, indignant that the girl should even think such a thing. "It is just that I promised Lenora——"

"Oh, come on," May said. "We will be back in an hour. You will have ample time to rehearse that last scene again. I won't let the ghosts hurt you," she promised laughingly.

"All right," Shirley said determinedly. May shouldn't think she was hanging back because of any fear of ghosts!

The two girls walked out College Avenue to where they cut through a thick growth of trees and underbrush that brought them out in front of the Mansion. The house was gray and forlorn in the April sunlight. Many of the windows were boarded up, and shutters hung awry on rusty hinges. The porch was rotting to decay, and the grass, where once had been a lovely garden, had grown into a miniature forest.

Shirley and May proceeded carefully and as silently as possible up to the front door and tried it. It swung open to their touch. Damp and musty air rushed out and met them. They entered and left the door standing open to let some light into the dark hallway. There was dust an inch thick on the floor, and tiny feet scurried away into dim recesses.

"Rats!" Shirley said eloquently.

"Where shall we go first?" May asked, trembling. She wished, now, that she hadn't insisted on coming here.

"We might as well look in all the rooms on the first floor," Shirley said. "Are you sure figures and lights were seen last night?"

"Yes," May nodded. "The soda clerk in Weller's told me several people had seen them."

"It doesn't look as though anyone had been in here for months," Shirley declared distastefully.

From one room to the other the girls went. Dust, inches thick and undisturbed, lay over everything. The house was just as it had been left when the smugglers were driven out last year. From their fruitless searchings of all the rooms on the first floor the girls turned back to the dark hall.

"Where do we go from here?" May quavered.

"We might as well go upstairs," Shirley said practically. "I don't think we will find any ghosts, though." It had been in her mind to distrust May when the girl insisted on coming out to the old house, but now Shirley's doubts were quelled. May wouldn't be as frightened as she seemed if there was nothing to her tale of ghosts.

The two mounted the stairs to the second floor and began a systematic search of the bedrooms. They came to a little room at the back of the hall. It was hardly bigger than a large closet, and in the corner was a pair of rickety steps leading up toward the ceiling.

"That trapdoor probably leads to the attic," Shirley said thoughtfully.

"Let's find out," May said, shivering in the darkness and dampness of the room. "You go first," she proposed as they moved toward the steps. "I don't want to come face to face with any ghosts."

"All right," Shirley laughed, "but it looks as though we will be disappointed. There don't seem to be any ghosts within a hundred miles."

"I—I hope not," May answered fervently.

Shirley mounted the steps, and they protested squeakingly under her weight. She put her shoulder against the trapdoor and lifted it. She peered into the darkness of the room above.

"There is nothing here."

"Go all the way up so I can come too," May said, starting up the steps behind Shirley.

Shirley climbed into the little attic room and stood up. It was as dark as night in here. The only faint glimmer of light in the place came from a broken skylight up in the ceiling. She turned to help May through the opening, and at that minute the trapdoor was slammed shut behind her. At first she thought it might have slammed accidentally, but May's taunting laugh proclaimed otherwise.

"Now, my dear Shirley, can you guess who will play the lead in the play tonight?" May laughed. "If the star doesn't appear, the understudy will go on in her place, and I know that the star won't appear."

"May!" Shirley tugged ineffectively at the trapdoor. "Let me out of here!"

"Tomorrow, darling, tomorrow. I am going to play Hamlet tonight."

"You won't," Shirley gritted.

"Oh, yes, I will. Let's see if your dear Alpha friends can find you now," May teased.

Her laugh floated up to Shirley as she made her way down the stairs. Shirley mentally harangued herself for ever coming a step away from the campus with May. She might have known the girl would be up to some trick. She had had this up her sleeve all the time she coaxed Shirley to come out to the Mansion. There never had been any ghosts and mysterious figures seen last night or any night this term. It was all part of May's plan to get Shirley interested. She knew a touch of mystery would intrigue Shirley, and then it would be easy to bring her to the old house. Why had she entered this room ahead of May? She could see now that the girl's fright had been merely assumed. May had known all the time that there were no ghosts to come face to face with.

She looked about her helplessly. What could she do? What would the girls think when she didn't come back to the Hall? What would they think when she didn't appear to play her part in tonight's performance? Would May really go on in the leading rôle? Would Lenora think she, Shirley, had stayed away deliberately? What would Beverly think? Oh, there must be some way out of this place! But she knew there wasn't. It was the same room in which Beverly had been a prisoner last year. Larry had rescued Beverly by pulling her up through the skylight, but nothing of the kind would happen now. Larry was in New York, and none of the Alpha girls had the faintest idea that Shirley was anywhere near the old house.

Would May return tomorrow morning as she had said and release Shirley from her prison? It seemed the only hope she had of getting out of the place. If May didn't return, what would happen to her? But she couldn't wait until tomorrow morning. The play was to go on tonight. She had to get out of here. She had the leading rôle, she couldn't throw her friends down. Hundreds of tickets had been sold. There would be lots and lots of people there. If May played the rôle of Hamlet she would make a mess of the whole play. But what could she, Shirley, do? She was a prisoner here with no means of escape. Shirley beat her hands impotently together and paced back and forth the narrow space of the room. Why couldn't she think of some means of escape? Somehow she had to outwit May! By some means she must return to the auditorium in time to play Hamlet when the play started. But how? How? That question haunted her. There were no windows in the room. There was no door but the trapdoor beneath her feet, and that was securely bolted from below.

CHAPTER XX

Hamlet Is Kidnaped

"Where is that girl?" Lenora demanded impatiently. "Half the afternoon is gone, and we still have this last scene to do."

"I don't understand it," Beverly declared. "Shirley should be here. She wouldn't stay away when it is so important."

"I hope she isn't still hunting for that old script," Lenora said.

The girls were in the auditorium waiting for Shirley to go on with the last scene. It was an hour since she had left them, to get her script. She had not reappeared, and at last Lois had departed in search of her. As yet, neither of the girls had returned.

"Can't find her any place," Lois announced breathlessly descending upon them. "I searched Chadwick Hall from roof to kitchen."

"That is strange," Anne declared. "Where could she have gone?"

"One of the sophomore girls said she saw Shirley going down College Avenue with May Norris," Lois volunteered.

"So what?" Lenora demanded.

"I don't know," Lois said frowning. "But if May Norris was with Shirley, there is something funny afoot."

"They're friends now," Beverly reminded the others.

"That's what you think," Lois said bluntly. "You will never make me believe that May is friendly toward any of the Alphas."

"You're right," Lenora agreed with Lois. "I wonder what she was up to?"

"Here she comes," Anne said in a whisper.

May entered the auditorium briskly and smiled jovially on all five.

"May, have you seen Shirley?" Lois demanded quickly.

"Why, I—yes. We walked in to Vernon together," May answered. "Shirley said she was going to Weller's."

May moved on then to the storeroom for something or other, and the girls she left exchanged mystified glances.

"Sounds screwy to me," Lois declared slangily, eloquently.

"Yes," Lenora nodded. "If it was true, why did she hesitate so before she told us?"

"And Shirley very seldom goes to Weller's alone," Beverly added.

"She wouldn't when she knew we were waiting for her," Anne continued.

Lenora dispatched Lois to find out if Shirley were in Weller's and turned back to the rest of the cast.

"We will just have to carry on as best we can without Shirley for a while," Lenora declared. "Hi, May," she called the other girl. "Come in here and play the part of Hamlet for the rehearsal of this last scene. You are only to play it now, not when the play goes on tonight," she explained. "Shirley will play it then."

"Very well," May answered, and the girls wondered why she smiled so slyly. Was she pleased merely to be playing the part at rehearsal?

Lois returned with the information that Shirley had not been near the ice-cream saloon all afternoon. Then where on earth could she be? She was not at the Hall and not at Weller's. They could think of no other place.

"At least she will be back for the play tonight,"

Lois said with more confidence than she felt.

"I hope so," Lenora declared. "If we have to put May in the leading rôle, the play will be a failure."

The girls returned to Chadwick Hall to await dinner. Dinner time came and went, and still no Shirley appeared. The girls were frankly worried. It was almost seven o'clock, and the play was to start at eight-fifteen. Where could Shirley be?

"Do you think she might have gotten stage fright and run away?" Lois asked hesitantly.

"Shirley wasn't afraid to face an audience," Lenora said firmly. "Look what a success she made of *Romeo and Juliet.*"

"Maybe she was kidnaped," Rosalie suggested.

"Hardly," Lenora scoffed. "But I can't understand why she doesn't appear. We have to go to the auditorium now and get into costumes."

Beverly was last to leave Chadwick Hall, and as she hurried across the campus to catch up with the other Alphas, two girls leaving Courtney Hall caught her eye. One was May Norris and the other girl was May's roommate.

"So you are to play the lead tonight, May?" the roommate was asking.

May laughed. "I'm the understudy, and Shirley won't come back tonight."

"How do you know?" demanded the other girl.

Yes, how did May know that Shirley would not appear to take her part in the play, Beverly wondered. Quite unabashedly she eavesdropped. It wasn't a polite thing to do, she realized, but who thinks of the polite things to do when one is curious? Something was wrong with Shirley, and May, from her smug attitude, knew all about it. Beverly meant to find out.

"Hamlet was kidnaped," May explained laughingly. "In fact, she almost kidnaped herself."

"What do you mean?" the roommate asked, bewildered. "I don't understand. How do you know what she did?"

"Because, my dear, I made her do it," May informed her roommate.

Beverly bristled to attention. So May did have something to do with Shirley's disappearance! Lois and Lenora had been right when they advised neither Beverly nor Shirley to trust her.

"Explain yourself," the other girl demanded.

"Promise you won't tell a soul," May said beseechingly. "Cross your heart."

When the roommate had fervently assured May that she would tell no living soul if only May would divulge the secret to her, May told her laughingly of the way she had tricked Shirley into the old house.

"And she is still there," finished May with delighted satisfaction. "She will stay there, too, until tomorrow morning. Tonight I will play the leading rôle. These Alpha girls have had things too much their own way on the campus. It is time someone made a few changes."

"But Shirley will tell Miss Wilder," the roommate declared. "Then what will you do?"

"I'll deny it," May said airily, "and I want you to back me up. Tell anyone who asks questions that I was with you all afternoon, except the time I was in the auditorium. Will you do it?"

"I don't know——"

"Come on, you might want some help yourself some day," May urged. "And think of Lenora's anger when she finds she has to put me in the leading rôle tonight."

"What if she doesn't give the part to you?" the other girl asked.

"She has to. All the seats are reserved, and the tickets are sold. They can't call the play off. I have to take Shirley's place."

"Do you think you can do it?"

"Of course I can—easily!" May said boastfully.

Beverly had her doubts. May would never be an actress—that is, not a truly great one. She thought too much of herself to be able to do justice to any part that was given her. The idea, locking Shirley in the attic of that old house! Beverly turned and ran back across the campus. Still running, she turned into College Avenue. She had to get to Shirley and let her out. Imagine May's surprise when Shirley appeared after all.

Beverly ran through the thick growth of trees and bounded up on the porch of the Mansion. The door was shut, and she pushed it open. The hall was pitch dark. She could not see a foot in front of her. It was good she knew her general way around in the old place. Her experiences last term had familiarized her with all the rooms. She felt her way to the stairs and ascended them. She mounted them, one by one. She stumbled badly over the top step, and the sound echoed like thunder along the empty hall. She went to the back room and walked into the closed door. If only it wasn't so dark in here!

She approached the steps leading up to the trap-door, and a familiar voice hailed her.

"Who's down there?"

"It's Beverly," she called back. In a second she had the trapdoor open, and Shirley descended like a miniature whirlwind.

"How did you find me? Did May tell you I was here? Has the play started yet? Where is May?"

"One at a time," Beverly said, laughing. "We have about twenty minutes to get to the auditorium before the play starts. We can settle with May afterward."

"You bet we will settle with her," Shirley said grimly. "She locked me in there, did you know? How did you find out where I was?"

"I overheard May telling her roommate about the trick she had played so she could play the leading rôle tonight."

"If only Lenora hasn't given it to her yet," Shirley wailed.

"I don't think she has," Beverly answered. "Lenora will hang on to the very last minute."

While they talked, the girls were making their way out of the Mansion. They turned into College Avenue and started forward at a brisk run.

CHAPTER XXI

Success

THE PEOPLE started arriving in the auditorium as early as seven forty-five. The orchestra did not put in its appearance until eight o'clock. They always supplied the musical interlude between eight and eight-fifteen, when the curtain rose. The orchestra was made up of girls from the college under the direction of the choral instructor.

In the seats out front everything was peaceful and pleasant as friends chatted and laughed agreeably together. But behind the scenes the members of the cast and their director were almost frantic.

"Where on earth can they be?" demanded Lenora, wringing her hands.

"You're asking me," wailed Lois. "If I knew, I'd go after them."

"You would not," Lenora said promptly. "No one leaves this stage until the play is over. Two of our cast are missing now, we don't want to lose any more!"

"What are we going to do?" asked Anne worriedly.

"I'll have to play the rôle of Hamlet," May suggested helpfully.

Lois and Lenora exchanged one of their lightning glances. Neither liked the smug complacency with which May had entered their midst. She seemed curiously self-assured tonight.

"But what about Beverly's part?" Rosalie asked. "She has no understudy."

"I wonder what ever possessed her to run off?" continued Lois.

"Perhaps she is with Shirley, wherever she is," suggested Lois, and wondered why May Norris looked so startled.

"There, the orchestra is starting its second piece," cried Lenora. "Oh, I'll never forget this night!"

"I don't think any of us will," added Anne. "How many minutes is it before the curtain rises?"

"Ten," Lenora groaned.

"The hour of our doom is near," declared Lois.

"Well," May Norris demanded, "am I to play the rôle of Hamlet? I have to have a few minutes to get into my costume."

Lenora sighed. "Yes, I suppose you will have to," she said unenthusiastically. Anyone could see at a glance that this was one of the hardest things Lenora had ever had to do. Where were Shirley and Beverly?

"Hold on there," a voice called from the door to the stage. "Nobody but me plays that part tonight."

"Shirley!"

"Beverly!"

The names were said with varied feelings. Lenora and the rest of the Alphas shouted them gayly, thankfully. But May Norris was utterly dumbfounded. She had been so sure of playing the leading rôle. How had Shirley managed to get away from the Mansion? The other girls scarcely noticed May's surprise in their joy at having Shirley back. But Shirley did not ignore the other girl. She flung May a meaning glance and a significant "I'll see you later."

The Alphas assisted their two recently returned members to struggle into their costumes.

"I haven't had any supper," Shirley wailed. "I'm half starved."

"I've brought some sandwiches," Lois produced them, "just in case——"

"A life saver!" Shirley declared.

"Hurry up," urged Lenora feverishly. "The curtain is about to go up. It would look funny to see Hamlet on the stage with a sandwich in her hand."

The others giggled approvingly. Finally Shirley and Beverly were in readiness, and not a minute too soon. The curtain went up, to the accompaniment of a burst of applause, and the first scene began. Lenora stood in the wings watching the players she had coached go through their parts. They knew their lines well, and each fairly lived the character she was playing.

"How're we doin'?" Lois demanded as the curtain rang down on the first act.

"Fair," Lenora said dryly. She refused to let the cast think for one minute that they were good. No one under her direction would ever become conceited with praise for her work. Lenora might appreciate them and think they were excellent, but she would never tell them so until the work was finished.

"Encouraging, aren't you?" Shirley drawled.

"Exactly," Lenora answered. "Now that we have a few minutes, let us hear what happened to you. And to you, Beverly."

Shirley explained minutely what had happened, ending with: "and there I was, fuming and gnashing my teeth, when Beverly appeared like an angel to deliver me from the rats and the dust."

In turn Beverly told how she had overheard May's conversation with her roommate and discovered where Shirley was.

"Of all the nerve," Lenora stormed. "May has more nerve than anyone I ever saw!"

"So that was what her friendship was leading up to," Lois nodded slowly. "I suspected her of something."

"There goes the second curtain," warned Lenora. "Scat!"

The girls hurried back to their positions overlooking the stage, and when their cues came entered and went through their scenes without a hitch. The audience fully appreciated the weeks of tedious work the girls had put in to perfect their parts and was generous with its applause. When the final curtain was down, the spectators cheered and applauded Shirley and Lois enthusiastically.

As Hamlet, Shirley had portrayed a really tragic character. She had brought to the rôle a fine understanding and sympathetic strain that captured the audience completely. Even Lois' fine portrayal of Ophelia was overshadowed by Shirley's really brilliant performance.

When the girls assembled in the dressing room to shed their costumes Lenora sank down in a chair exhausted.

"I never thought you would do it," she confessed. "I was in hot water every minute."

"I wouldn't go through it again for a million dollars," Beverly declared fervently. It had been her first experience before a college audience, and she devoutly vowed it would be her last. She would leave theatricals to her dramatically inclined friends. Never would they inveigle her into accepting another part in any of their productions.

"What's the matter?" Lois laughed. "Were you scared?"

"Oh," Beverly said eloquently, "when I got out there and saw all those people, I could have fallen through the floor!"

"That was your first experience," Shirley smiled. "After a while you won't mind it a bit."

"I won't take any more parts," Beverly declared. "I'm through with dramatics."

"You did fine," Lenora assured her.

"How about the rest of us?" asked Lois, unashamedly angling for compliments.

"Beyond words," Lenora giggled.

The members of the cast departed one by one until only the six Alphas were left. They were in no hurry to return to Chadwick Hall, so they sat about chatting together. A knock sounded on the dressing-room door.

"They have come to throw us out," Lois declared. "We shouldn't have stayed here so long."

"As long as we don't get locked in," Anne said, and stopped.

The Dean and a gentleman, no member of the faculty, stood there in the doorway. The girls jumped to their feet.

"Girls, this is Mr. Forsythe, manager of the Forsythe Film Company. Mr. Forsythe, these are the members of one of the most popular sororities on the campus—the Alpha Delta girls. Girls," the Dean continued, "Mr. Forsythe has been looking over the college grounds, and he wants to make a motion picture here next term."

The girls exchanged wondering glances.

"And," the director added, "I will bring the star of the picture from Hollywood, but there will be minor rôles to be taken by the girls of the school. When I suggested this to Miss Wilder, she at once told me about the actresses who were to take part tonight. I decided to stay over and see the play, and may I compliment each one of you on the fine performance you gave?"

Of course, there was more conversation exchanged about the proposed picture before the Dean and Mr. Forsythe departed, but the girls were too excited and thrilled to do more than grasp the main points. One thing stood out clearly above the others: the film company was to make a motion picture right here on the campus next term, and the girls would all have a chance before the camera. Of course, their parts wouldn't amount to much, but even the prospect of seeing a picture in the throes of production was thrilling. And to have a real star from Hollywood living in their midst——

"Won't it be grand?" murmured Lois.

"Splendiferous!" Lenora declared.

"I wonder if there will be a handsome leading man?" continued the irrepressible Lois.

"What do you care?" teased Shirley. "You won't be able to get within a mile of him."

"Let's report the news to the rest of the Chadwick Hall girls," proposed Anne.

"Good idea!" sang out Lenora. "I'll be the first one outside!"

The girls raced hastily for the door, shouting and laughing as they ran through the auditorium. They were brought up short at the front doors.

"Locked!" wailed Lenora. "Do we have to stay in here all night?"

"Try the back doors," suggested Beverly practically.

They went back past the dressing rooms to the back doors. One was unlocked, and they proceeded to pile out into the fresh air.

"Just a minute," Shirley called. "Did anyone put out the light in the dressing room?"

"I don't think so," answered Lois.

"I'll go back," Shirley said, and ran back into the building. She was on her way to the dressing room that the Alphas had shared when something gave her pause. Little wafts of smoke were curling from under the door that May Norris and several other girls had shared. "Beverly! Lenora! Lois! Come quickly!" Shirley shouted and turned the knob of the door.

"What—is the matter?" gasped Lenora and the others as they ran back to her.

"Look!" Shirley pointed significantly to the smoke that was increasing in volume. "The room must be on fire—and the door is locked!"

"What will we do?" Anne shivered.

"Break it in," said Beverly and Lenora together.

"Come on, girls," Shirley directed, "put your shoulders to the panel. Now, altogether, one—two —three-e-e-e!"

The lock was not made to resist much pressure

and readily gave under the combined weight of
four of the Alpha girls. The smoke rushed out at
them and gave them pause on the threshold. Immediately Beverly and Shirley ran for fire extin-
guishers and applied them. The flames were stubborn, but they had not made much headway.
Gradually the fire sizzled out, leaving nothing but
water-soaked ashes.

"Well," Lenora said with satisfaction, "that was
quick work. Three cheers for the Alpha Deltas!"

"But how did it start?" Rosalie asked in concern.
"There was no one in here."

"Not at the moment," Shirley said. She walked
over to what had once been a new lacquered dressing table. Now it was scarred and burnt from the
flames. She picked up a tin ash tray and held it
out for the other girls' inspection. "It is plain,
isn't it, how the fire started?"

"Evidently you mean someone left a lighted
cigarette in the ash tray. Probably on a piece of
paper or something," answered Anne.

"Exactly," Shirley said. "And who, of the girls
who had this dressing room, smokes?"

"May Norris," replied Lois significantly.

"She always was careless," added Rosalie.

"The fire might have destroyed the whole building if we hadn't caught it in time," Lenora said.

"Do you think we should tell Miss Wilder?" Anne asked after a moment during which the girls stared from one to the other in silence.

"We will tell her about the fire," Beverly answered, "but——"

"And we will tell her about May, too," Lois declared. "You know and I know that the Dean doesn't like the girls to smoke. May deliberately disobeyed, and look what might have happened. As it is, the dressing room is a wreck!"

"May has been inviting trouble all term," added Lenora. "Now she can take what is coming to her."

"Because you tell on her," Beverly said.

"Do you want us to keep quiet about such a thing?" demanded Lois. "It is serious."

"I know it is," Beverly acknowledged, "but we cannot be sure that it was May who is responsible."

"None of the other girls smoke," Shirley put in. "That is, none who shared this dressing room with her."

"I vote we tell Miss Wilder," Lois insisted. "It is only fair that she should know what May has been doing these past few months."

"Don't you think she knows?" Beverly asked. "She sees what is going on about the campus. If the news of May's smoking came up before the faculty board, she would be expelled. She is in bad enough with them as it is."

"And you want us to protect her?" Rosalie demanded.

Beverly shook her head. "I only want you to be fair. You really don't know that it was May who caused the fire."

"I'm going to find out," Shirley said grimly.

"Where are you going?" Beverly asked quickly.

"I'm going to see May Norris and tell her what has happened."

"But——" began Beverly.

"It is no use," Shirley said stormily. "I won't let her slide out of this. She has gotten away with too many things this past term." It was the nearest she and Beverly had ever come to quarreling, and Beverly recognized the fact that in this thing Shirley could not be swayed. The other girls were with Shirley, too. Perhaps it would do May good, teach her a lesson, if they were to confront her with the news of what her carelessness had led to.

"We'll all come along and see the dear girl," Lenora said sweetly.

They left the auditorium building and proceeded across the campus to Courtney Hall. Most of the girls were in bed, and they proceeded into the building and up the stairs on tiptoe, lest they disturb the house mistress. They were all fighting mad. None of the Alphas had ever really liked May Norris, and now they were all set against her. That the girl could be so careless, and that her carelessness might have resulted in a tragedy, did not serve in any way as balm to their anger. They were firmly resolved that after talking to May they would go at once to Miss Wilder and acquaint her with what had happened.

They knocked on May's door, but no one answered. Deliberately Lenora turned the knob, and the Alphas entered. May was there, but her roommate was not. The girl was evidently in one of the other rooms, making merry. So much the better; they would have May all to themselves.

"What do you want?" May was sitting up in bed.

"We want to talk to you," Shirley said, acting as spokesman for the group.

May looked from one serious face to the other. "Well?" she demanded. "Say what you have to say and leave my room."

"We didn't come here on a pleasure visit," cut in Lenora. "It might pay you to be polite, at least."

"I suppose you have come to have revenge for my locking you in the attic of the Mansion," May said to Shirley, tossing her head defiantly.

"No," Shirley said calmly. "We aren't here because of that."

This answer plainly astounded May. She could think of no other reason for the Alphas to pay her a visit.

"What do you want, then?" she demanded sullenly.

"You are in the habit of smoking, aren't you?" Shirley asked.

"What is that to you?" May demanded.

"A lot," Lenora answered. "To you it means more than you guess right now."

"Well, say what you have to say," May said, sinking back languorously on her pillows. "I suppose you have come to give me a puritan lecture."

"We haven't come to lecture," Shirley said, checking her temper with an effort. She wanted to shake May, she was so indolent. "Tonight you were smoking in the dressing room back stage, weren't you?"

"So what? Are you going to tell Miss Wilder?" May inquired lazily.

"We might," Lois admitted.

May sat up and regarded them intently. "Just what is all this leading up to?"

"To this," Shirley said quickly, "tonight you went out of the dressing room and left a lighted cigarette. The room caught fire. The building might have burned down if we hadn't checked the flames."

"So you checked them," May sneered. "The brave Alphas to the rescue!"

Lenora started forward indignantly, but Beverly held her back.

"Evidently you don't realize the seriousness of your offense," Shirley continued. "Perhaps you will in the morning, when Miss Wilder calls you to her office."

May grasped Shirley's arm in a tense grip. "You told her that I was to blame? But you aren't sure! You can't be sure that it was my fault."

"I'm as sure that it was your fault as I am sure that you are here now," Shirley insisted. "You were the only girl of those in that dressing room who smoked. There is no one else to blame."

"But think of what it will mean," May pleaded wildly. "She will expel me."

"That is your worry," cut in Lenora heartlessly.

"You should have thought of that before you started smoking," added Lois.

"Think of my parents and my friends," May cried. "What will they think if I am expelled?"

"You think of 'em," returned Lenora. "They are your affair."

"But you can't do this thing," May insisted. "I didn't know my cigarette was lighted. I never thought that the room might catch fire."

"That is just it," Shirley rebuked, "you never thought! You don't think about a thing but your own selfish ends. You know Miss Wilder doesn't like the girls in college to smoke, yet you deliberately disobeyed her and instigated other girls to do the same. If Vernon was run by girls of your kind it would be a wreck within a week. Why don't you try, at least for the rest of your college life, to be the kind of girl this school wants you to be?"

The Alphas regarded their victim in hostile silence. May looked from one to the other and saw friendship in none of them.

"I won't smoke again," she promised faithfully. "Don't tell Miss Wilder about this, and I promise never to touch another cigarette while I'm at Vernon," she added.

"Until we are out of sight," said Lois. "Do you think you could keep a promise?"

May was utterly humble now. She did not fly into a rage at Lois' implied insult. She knew that the Alphas would do as they threatened. She had only one chance to make them see that she was sincere.

"How do we know you will keep your word?" Shirley asked. Her temper was abating somewhat, and she was beginning to regret having come here. They should have gone directly to Miss Wilder and let her deal with the situation—and May.

"I promise I won't," May said beseechingly. "I know I haven't been the right kind of a student. I've broken a lot of rules and regulations—and I'm sorry, truly I am. I didn't dream that my carelessness might have serious results."

"You are an upper classman," Shirley reminded her, "and what kind of an example are you setting for the new students? They see you breaking rules and laughing at the traditions of Vernon—they will do the same. It is no way to start their college life."

"I know." May was thoroughly miserable now. "Go ahead and tell Miss Wilder, if you want to," she said slowly. "I don't care if she does expel me. I suppose I'm not good enough to stay a student at Vernon."

Beverly stepped forward then. "I think this has gone far enough. We aren't going to tell Miss Wilder tonight, May. We will give you a chance to— reform and be the kind of girl you should be. If you go back to your old ways, though, we shall tell her promptly. The whole situation is up to you."

With that ultimatum the Alphas left May to think over what they had said. They went to Miss Wilder's office and told her of the fire in the dressing room, but not one of them mentioned May's name in connection with it. They would keep their word and see if she really did change, as she had promised. After seeing Miss Wilder they returned to Chadwick Hall and tumbled into bed for a much needed peaceful rest.

CHAPTER XXII

Farewell

IT WAS JUNE again, and time to part for the summer vacation. As was customary on the last day of the term, the Alphas were holding their meeting. They were met in Shirley's and Beverly's room, their usual rendezvous.

Beverly and Shirley were perched jauntily on the window sill, while the other four members of the Alpha Delta Sorority lounged on the beds or on lavish pillows on the floor.

Beverly, much to her own surprise and the delight of the other Alphas, had been elected president of her class. That meant that she was the president of the next graduating class. She had been quite astounded at her popularity, and secretly thrilled and humble that the girls should consider her worthy of leading them. It was a responsible position, and Beverly clearly recognized that fact. She hoped sincerely that she would be able to live up to her classmates' expectations of her. She couldn't understand, in the first place, why the girls had elected her. She felt that there were others much better suited for the position.

The girls were discussing Beverly's new position as they chatted on this their last night of the junior term.

"Yes, ma'am," Lenora declared to all and sundry, "the Alpha Delta Sorority should feel mighty proud to have the class president in their ranks."

"I can't understand why they elected me," Beverly said smiling.

The other girls looked at the slim, brown-haired girl before them, the girl with the clear, steady blue eyes and gently molded features. They fully appreciated her sweetness and charm and were ruled by it. They understood why she had been elected to lead them through their last year of college life. She was so typically the American College Girl. Her warm-heartedness and sense of fair play and good sportsmanship had won for her an army of friends. It was no wonder, when everyone loved her, that she should have been chosen as their leader. It would have been more to wonder at if she hadn't.

"What," Lois demanded, "isn't the noble Lenora going to make a speech on this our last night?"

"If you insist," Lenora said jumping up immediately. "Unaccustomed as I am to public speaking——"

"Wait a minute," Lois said pulling Lenora back beside her on the bed, "nobody insisted that you speak. In fact, it is a relief to see you silent for once in your life."

"Oh, but you really couldn't leave without a speech from me," declared Lenora modestly.

"Just give us the chance, just give us the chance," begged Lois.

"No," Lenora insisted. "I must make my speech."

"See what you started," Shirley frowned on Lois. "Why did you mention a speech in the first place?"

"Did I know what it would lead to?" demanded Lois. "I have just as big a headache as you have."

"Let's have some lemonade while Lenora prepares her speech," proposed Anne.

"It will take away the bad effect," added Rosalie wickedly.

The girls set about preparing the lemonade, and when it was made they settled down resignedly with a cool, tinkling glassful to listen to Lenora's inevitable speech.

"Come on, get it over with," Lois said sipping her liquid refreshment.

"The dinner bell will ring in a moment," continued Shirley.

"I'm not going to make a speech," Lenora said slowly.

"You're—not——" Lois looked at her friend helplessly. "Are you sick? What makes you refuse such a golden opportunity?"

Lenora grinned. "I haven't anything to say," she replied.

"That didn't stop you before," Lois declared.

"Instead——" began Lenora.

"Ah, I knew there was a catch in it somewhere," murmured the mischievous Lois.

"Instead," continued Lenora imperturbably, "I propose a toast."

"Hear! Hear!" cried Shirley as the girls jumped to their feet and held their glasses high.

"Wherever you go," Lenora began, "whatever you do, may life always hold a smile for you!"

"So be it!" the others echoed.

Here let us take leave of Beverly and the other Alpha girls for a while. But we shall meet with them again in *Beverly Gray, Senior,* when the Forsythe Film Company will make a motion picture at Vernon, and the girls will meet with some new and exciting adventures.